In the Absence
of Absalon

Simon Okotie was born in London to a Nigerian father and an English mother. He lives in Norfolk.

SIMON OKOTIE

IN THE ABSENCE OF ABSALON

LONDON

PUBLISHED BY SALT PUBLISHING 2017

2 4 6 8 10 9 7 5 3 1

Copyright © Simon Okotie 2017

First published in Great Britain in 2017 by
Salt Publishing Ltd
International House, 24 Holborn Viaduct, London EC1A 2BN United Kingdom

www.saltpublishing.com

Salt Publishing Limited Reg. No. 5293401

A CIP catalogue record for this book is available from the British Library

ISBN 978 1 78463 102 4 (Paperback edition)
ISBN 978 1 78463 103 1 (Electronic edition)

Typeset in Neacademia by Salt Publishing

Printed and bound in Great Britain by Clays Ltd, St Ives plc

For
Danayutta

IN THE ABSENCE OF ABSALON

H IS PERCEPTIONS SHOULD, he thought, be full of
the architectural and other pertinent details of the townhouse before him. This was to enable those less senior than
himself to reconstruct the scene for themselves, in their own
minds, as a means of trying to piece together the circumstances
surrounding the disappearance of his colleague, Marguerite.
He knew, then, that he should be making appropriate observations available to his subordinates concerning the physical
appearance of the townhouse and its interior, particularly given
its proximity to the last known sighting of Marguerite and
its connection with Harold Absalon, the Mayor's transport
advisor, whose disappearance the former had been investigating
prior to his own disappearance. Why, then, this restraint on
his part, he wondered, as he noted the number plate of the car
parked haphazardly, facing in the wrong direction, in the street
outside the house? Did he have evidence to suggest that the
building was not, in fact, central to his investigation despite
this confluence of circumstances? Or was it that, despite its
centrality, he had decided not to describe it to avoid com-
promising what was, after all, a live investigation? A further
alternative was that, regardless of the building's centrality or
otherwise to his investigation, he was refraining from describing it through what's known as absentmindedness or through a
deliberate attempt to frustrate the expectations of those trained
in the classical and, granted, some more modern schools of

investigation. All of the foregoing could, of course, be just a momentary restraint – just a way, in other words, for him to move towards revealing the details of the building and its interior, a mental clearing of the throat, so to speak, before the revelation of what some felt needed to be revealed. And this was not to exhaust all of the possibilities, he noted with regret.

As he traversed the short distance that separated him from the gate leading to the area in front of the townhouse as a precursor, he hoped, to opening it and moving towards the building proper, he realised that part of the reason for his reticence in describing the architectural and other pertinent details of the townhouse before him related to a hitherto unarticulated pressure to do so: he felt an intense – and intensifying – pressure arising from a source or sources unknown which, momentarily, was making his mind – and hence this report – a blank, at least in relation to conveying, through whatever means mysterious to him, the architectural and other details previously alluded to. He was becoming increasingly aware, then, of how much was resting on his shoulders, would be another formulation. And the reason, he realised, that a lot was resting on those parts of his anatomy was that, if his subordinates, those with access to these case notes, were to be able to follow his investigation, then he would surely need to record – need, at least, to notice – all of the pertinent features of the building in all of their detail. Now his training – and mentoring by his colleague Marguerite – must have given him an exceptional grounding in the types of details to be noticed and how to notice them; he was satisfied that, were he left to his own devices, as it is known, he would be able to take in those details and use them effectively to continue to unearth the circumstances of his erstwhile mentor's disappearance whilst in pursuit of Harold Absalon. But he was, somehow, increasingly aware that he was not alone. He had a strong suspicion that others, like ourselves, were breathing down his neck. And that, he thought, was part of what was giving him pause; how, in short, could he know that what he took to be pertinent - and hence what he made a mental note of - would seem pertinent to all (or some) of the budding (and, granted, some more senior) detectives who were somehow following his investigation into Marguerite's disappearance and who, in fact, wanted to solve the mystery of that disappearance before he himself had done so? How could he know, in other words, that we would accede to what he took to be descriptively remarkable, to put it in that new way? He couldn't, was his conclusion, and that was why he refrained - it was too great a burden. The responsibility he felt resting so heavily upon his shoulders, that being the part of the anatomy where heavy items of a material nature tended to reside when being carried in such circumstances, felt, in short, to be insupportable; he was to provide sufficient and appropriate detail about the building in question to allow one or more of the less experienced detectives following in his footsteps as it were and with access, somehow (he wouldn't go into that now), to his mental case notes and files, to make a name for him- or herself, as it is known in some quarters, by solving the mystery of the disappearance of Marguerite, last seen in pursuit of Harold Absalon, the Mayor's transport advisor, before anyone else - including himself - had done so. He felt it to be impossible. He did not want to influence people through his selective perceptions. Nor did he want to stand in the way of someone at an earlier stage of their investigative career who wanted to make a name for themselves in this way, whether they were male or female and regardless of whether they wanted to make that name known to all and sundry or wanted to keep it to themselves – as he, himself, seemed to be doing – as a way of remaining undercover, in other words, as an aid, no doubt, to solving further mysteries and to unearthing further circumstances surrounding the disappearance of people regardless of whether those people were themselves experienced investigators, advisors to the Mayor, both or neither. He did not want to stand in the way of people, then, and it was perhaps for that further reason that he did not describe, which is to say he did not think about, the distinctive and pertinent architectural and other features of the townhouse which he continued to approach, pursuers bearing down upon him from left and right, the street behind him quiet because it was, perhaps, the middle – or thereabouts – of the night.

But wasn't refraining from describing the relevant distinctive features of the building, to reformulate it in that way, a means, actually, of standing in the way of the very people he was trying to help? Wasn't he interposing himself, in fact, between those wanting to make a name for themselves by unearthing, before him, the circumstances surrounding the disappearance of his colleague Marguerite? Was he not using himself as a way of blocking people's view of those very details? Surely if he was ensuring that he wasn't in the way of others then those others would be able to see *all* of the distinctive architectural and other features of the building in question. But this didn't take account of the burden he was carrying, remember (in the usual place), a burden that took the form of being the eyes and ears (and, he hoped, in relation to certain individuals, the lips and tongue) of the whole mass of people wishing to solve the crime, if one had been committed, before he himself had done so.

4

Was there something disingenuous in his thinking in this way, then, he now wondered, as he removed his gloved hands from his jacket pockets in readiness for the next phase of his investigation? Surely he knew that actually his job was to provide just sufficient detail, just enough clues, for him to stay one step ahead of those trying to look over his shoulder, as it were. He knew, surely, that he was involved in an elaborate dance with the great mass of people trying to solve the case before him. That, presumably, was what he wanted *and* what they wanted, namely the satisfaction of him staying just one step ahead of them at all times. Given that he could not conceive of how anyone could be so close as to be able to look over his shoulder in the way that you yourself are doing (particularly given the burden he is supposedly carrying there) and that he was describing the scenes before him as best he could (and maybe he'd simply missed the architectural module of his training), he refused to countenance the existence of any such game, any such desire on his part to stay one step ahead of you or any other budding detective wishing to get one over on him, as it were. In short, he was just not that interested in the appearance of the building. He just didn't think, at that moment, that any of its features were that distinctive, except perhaps that the gate barring him, as it were, from the area in front of the townhouse had a padlocked chain around it. He did not think that any of the architectural features were pertinent, perhaps, to his investigation into Marguerite's disappearance; at least he thought them impertinent, as it were, at that moment, which is not to say that he wouldn't volunteer important detail as he continued to approach the building in question, such as the observation that there was a small step protruding from beneath the gate leading to the area in front of the townhouse, that the gate was surmounted by ornamental spikes, as were the area railings of which it was, as it were, a part, that the area railings were mounted upon a dwarf wall, that there was a short flight of stairs to the left, leading up to the front door of the townhouse, and another, to the right, leading down to a basement, that the townhouse consisted of five storeys, in total, including the basement, and that he had, he hoped, in his right-hand trouser pocket, a key to the padlock – and to the house – a bunch, in fact, that belonged to a colleague of Harold Absalon's, a colleague, moreover, called Richard Knox whom Harold Absalon had fallen out with, as it is known, shortly before his disappearance, and whose family had been in possession of this townhouse for generations.[1]

1 I took the opportunity, in Absalon's absence, of insinuating myself into Knox's company. I thought it wouldn't do my prospects any harm, although this didn't mean I now trusted him.

2

A SAFE HOUSE was safe, he surmised, to the extent that its whereabouts were unknown to those intent on causing harm to the occupants or potential occupants of that house. He could not, then, refer to the townhouse in front of him as a safe house at that moment: clearly his pursuers would be able to see him entering the house, were he to do so after going through the padlocked, ornamentally spiked gate and through the area in front of the townhouse; they would, then, know his whereabouts at that moment, the whereabouts of the house in question and, through the application of rudimentary logic, his whereabouts in relation to the house – namely, inside it – and to that extent the house would cease, if it ever had been, to be a safe house, which is to say it would cease to be a safe house for him and possibly for any or all of its other inhabitants or potential inhabitants. This was why, quite simply, he could not bring himself to refer to the townhouse towards which he continued to move, by placing his left foot, in advance of his right, against the step that protruded from beneath the gate leading to the area in front of the townhouse, as a safe house.

He had, though, started to view the area in *front* of the townhouse as a potential place of safety. Why was this, he wondered, as he removed his right-hand glove from his right hand as a precursor to retrieving the keys from the equivalent trouser pocket? The reason that he had started to view the area in this way was, he thought, precisely because he had that key and could, if he wished, on entering the area, simply lock the gate behind him with the added flourish of breaking the key in the padlock, thereby preventing any of his pursuers who had in their possession a key to the same padlock from using that key to unlock the padlock as a precursor to continuing to pursue him. He could, in other words, use a trick that he'd been taught in cadet school of opening the padlock, removing it from the chain securing the gate, opening the gate, entering the area, closing the gate, wrapping the chain securely around the gate and railings again, relocking the padlock without re-moving the key and then breaking the key in the lock such that part of the key would remain hidden in the lock, thereby preventing anyone else with a key from inserting it into the padlock in the appropriate place as a means of opening the padlock again, or of using that part of his key that remained in the padlock, which is to say that part of the key that he had used to open the padlock that remained in the padlock, to open the padlock; and this trick was a means of making the area safe – safer, at least, than it would otherwise have been – and this despite the fact his pursuers would be able to see him within that area.

But he didn't want to use this trick in this way to produce this outcome – that was why he had referred to the area in front of the townhouse only as a *potential* rather than as an actual place of safety. The reason that he didn't want to and would not use this trick of breaking the key in the padlock was not to do with his distrust of the occupants of the building in question, although he did distrust them. Nor was his avoidance of this trick a means of avoiding trapping himself in the house or area in question. No, the reason that he would not break the key in the padlock was because he wanted to allow his pursuers access to the area in question and, beyond that, access to the house itself, were he to secure such access. And he wanted one of his pursuers in particular to secure such access, and that was Harold Absalon.

3

H E PLACED HIS foot - the right - upon the small step that protruded from beneath the gate leading to the area in front of the townhouse, and immediately wondered whether the main advantage of doing so, which was that it would facilitate access to his right-hand trouser pocket, would, in fact, outweigh the main disadvantage, which was that it would constrict that pocket, thereby making it more difficult to withdraw the key that he hoped was contained therein. Why, he now wondered, had he only commenced this line of inquiry into the action in question upon completing it? Would it not, in retrospect, have been better to initiate and even complete this analysis in advance of the action, as a means of determining whether it was, in fact, the best course at that stage, particularly given the fine margins separating success from failure in such investigations?

What he realised, as he lifted the heel of the foot that he'd placed upon that step, was that he could not have known that placing his foot in this position would have tightened the aperture and interior of the pocket in question to the extent that it had. Further evidence had, in short, become available to him during the course of his action, evidence to suggest that the main advantage of it, which was to reduce the distance between his right hand and the equivalent trouser pocket, may, in fact, be outweighed by the main disadvantage, which was that the same action - that of placing his foot - the right - upon the small step that protruded from beneath the gate leading to the area in front of the townhouse – would constrict the right-hand pocket of his trousers wherein he hoped lay the key, literally and metaphorically, respectively, to the padlock securing that gate and to solving, or resolving, the mystery, if there was (or is) one, surrounding the disappearance of Marguerite, his investigative colleague, who was last seen on the trail of Harold Absalon, the Mayor's transport advisor, who had been missing, and, in so doing, act as impediment to retrieving that key, thereby potentially preventing him from entering the area in front of the townhouse prior to being apprehended by those wishing to thwart his investigation.

The benefit, then, of bringing that pocket and thus (he hoped) the key closer to his right hand by placing the equivalent (to call it that) foot on the step that protruded from beneath the gate leading to the area in front of the townhouse as a means of facilitating the key's – and the related hand's – removal from that pocket (this simultaneous withdrawal not being a coincidence, of course, in that the hand in question – the right – would, he hoped, be clasping the key, and it would be for that reason that they would emerge from the pocket simultaneously, or near simultaneously, in this scenario) could, he now thought, given the new evidence that had, as it were, come into his possession, be outweighed by the increased constriction of that pocket brought about – to specify this for the first time – by the fact that the right leg had bent, at the knee, in this manoeuvre, an action that, through applying pressure to the interior of the trouser leg, had tautened the material from which that trouser leg had been fashioned, thereby causing any pockets within that material to be constrained, resulting in it being increasingly difficult, he realised, in retrospect, as he continued to elevate the heel of the foot – the right – so as to bring the equivalent pocket ever closer to that hand, thereby tautening the pocket still further, to retrieve objects, such as keys, from those pockets.

What, then, was this new piece of evidence that had, as it were, come into his possession to suggest that the main advantage of placing his right foot at an elevated position in relation to his left and to use the step that protruded from beneath the gate leading to the area in front of the townhouse as the means of achieving this, in other words by placing that foot – the right – on that step whilst refraining from placing the left at a similar elevated position on that step – leaving, in short, the left foot in its original position, as it were, on the pavement or sidewalk – which was that the key or keys in question, which, remember, he believed to be contained within his right-hand trouser pocket and which he wished to retrieve from that trouser pocket as a precursor to facilitating entry to the area in front of the townhouse by using it or them to unlock the padlock securing the gate leading to that area, would be placed, internally within the pocket this was (but not in relation to the pocket), at a slightly elevated position compared to that in which it or they would have been placed had he not moved the foot on that side – the right – onto the step that protruded from beneath the gate leading to the area in front of the townhouse, a slight advantage – that of the increased height of the keys in relation, most importantly, to the hand on that side – the right – if not in relation to the pocket containing them – that was as it were supported by a subsidiary advantage that he now adumbrated for the first time: that of moving the key, and the pocket, forwards slightly, thereby taking them closer to the gate leading to the area in front of the townhouse, may, in fact, be outweighed, as it were, by the main disadvantage of placing that foot on the pediment in question, if the definition of pediment is broad enough, and his memory and deployment of it accurate enough, to encompass and incorporate the step that protruded (as before), which was that this action on his part would also constrict somewhat the pocket from which he hoped to retrieve the keys that would, he believed, unlock the gate to the area in front of the townhouse as well, he hoped, as the door to the townhouse itself? The evidence, in short, that had, as it were, come into his possession at the moment that he'd placed his foot - the right - in the aforementioned position was, quite simply, that he was wearing a different, tighter pair of trousers to those he'd thought he was wearing when he had initiated this action, meaning that any pocket within those trousers would, upon placing one foot at an elevated position in relation to the other (thereby necessitating the bending of the leg connected to that elevated foot) be more constricted than it would have been had he been wearing his other, looser, trousers, making it more difficult, as before, to retrieve items, such as keys, from that pocket.

What, though, he now wondered, as his hand - the right - finally, with difficulty, entered the upper reaches, as it were, of his right-hand trouser pocket, if the key to the padlock was, in fact, contained in the trousers he'd worn, turn and turn about, one day previously?

4

H E PONDERED, FOR a moment, whether, in fact, he still had another, looser, pair of trousers and, if he did, where he'd changed from those trousers into the ones he was currently wearing. He must surely, he thought, have a home to go to, as it was so often put, particularly by the landladies of the public houses that he hardly ever had the funds or the inclination to patronise, and one in which he was not only able to change from these trousers into his other pair, or vice versa in the case where he was in fact wearing the other pair and wanted to change into this pair, a home where he must also be able to store this or his other pair of trousers but not both at the same time, since this would imply, in the case where he had no more and no fewer than two pairs of trousers in his possession, that he had gone out without wearing either of them (something he often wondered and worried about when he was actually out on the streets in the course of his investigations but which, hitherto, he had not done - namely, left his home, assuming, for now, that he had one to go to, without having put on either pair of his trousers, or, to put it another way, without having put on either one of his pair of pairs of trousers).

But what if, in answer to the publicly expressed question (a question, moreover, he thought, as he slid the ball of his right foot back towards himself, that was often publicly expressed in the public bar of the public house) of the public house landladies of that land, the one that related to whether the men, typically, therein, did, or did not, have homes to go to, he did not, in fact, have a home to go to? What if, through some misadventure the details of which had, for whatever reason, slipped his mind, he had no home? It would not help him, he thought, to answer the question of the public house landlady in the negative, a question which, as before, must be publically expressed, whether in the public or in a more private bar, in the land that he inhabited or had inhabited at the time the question was posed, and the reason it would not help him to answer in the negative the public house landlady's question about whether or not he and others therein had homes to go to in the situation where he, in fact, for one, had no home to go to related to the difference, perhaps, between a house and a home, with the latter being a private residence where one could place one's pairs of trousers, in the situation where one had more than one pair, and also, in that situation, change from one pair to another (or, where one only had a pair of pairs of trousers, which is to say, where one only had four trousers in total, change from one pair to *the* other pair), whereas a house, and particularly a *public* house, was not a private place nor was it a residence, except, in many instances, for the pub landlady and her family, were she to have one, as the name implied (and even a private bar in a public house was not private in the sense that a home was private) and would only, in fact, be open to the public between certain circumscribed hours that were in large part dependent on the licensing laws extant in that land at that point in its history.

The only situation in which answering in the negative the public house landlady's question, a question that was often expressed loudly, and certainly publicly, regardless of whether it was expressed loudly and publicly in a lounge, private or public bar, was, he noted, as the ball of that foot neared the edge of the step, in the situation where the public house landlady was a single woman with whom there had already been a mutual sexual frisson[2] - between him and her, this was - during the course of that evening or a number of evenings or daytimes, depending on the licensing laws extant in that land at that point in its history, to the extent that, when the other punters had gone, singly, collectively, or in droves, to the homes that she - the public house landlady located in a public house that he and she were then, and/or are currently residing in - had enquired about in the public, loud and, most must realise, rhetorical way previously referred to, regardless of the precise nature of the bar in that public house within which the question had been raised, she might invite him upstairs for what's known as a nightcap. But that situation did not often occur for the simple reason that most public house landladies were married, which is to say that most public house landladies had a public house landlord in tow, as it were, a public house landlord who often left it to their landlady wives to ask their guests, to call them that, and only at the appropriate moment, whether they had homes to go to, since this question was probably easier to take from a woman, given that, coming from a woman it would add something of the feminine touch that was, so often, a large part of what differentiated a house from a home. And it was for this reason that the situation of a single, in the sense of being romantically and sexually unattached, public house landlady having asked the question - of him and others - about whether he had a home to go to and him responding to the

2 Obviously I would need to keep the affair with Absalon's wife from Knox, and not just because of his own reputation. It would, of course, cause ructions within the project office, were it to become widely known, and that would surely impede my progress.

question in the negative, having established a romantic and even sexual, although, as yet, unconsummated rapport with that single (in the sense defined) public house landlady during the course of that evening or a number of evenings and afternoons (depending, as before) in the hope of being taken from that public, private, or lounge bar upstairs into the decidedly private lounge or bedroom of the home, note, of that single public house landlady with, perhaps, the intention of becoming a public house landlord, in time, and having the opportunity then, oneself, of asking whether or not they had homes to go to, in the situation when one did not, for whatever reason, defer the responsibility for asking that question to one's wife, the public house landlady, was a rare one, he thought, as he lowered the heel of his right foot, which was now, as it were, overhanging the edge of the step, to release, somewhat, the constriction in the equivalent trouser pocket and allow his hand – the right – to plunge, finally, into its depths.

5

O F T H E T W O pairs of trousers he seemingly owned, as well as one being tighter than the other, one was more worn than the other, which was not to say that he wore that pair more frequently than the other – it has already been established that he wore the two pairs of trousers in his possession turn and turn about – but to say that that pair (which happened, also, to be the tighter pair) was more worn than the other pair in the sense that they were more worn down, although the fact that they were more worn down didn't necessarily mean that they had been worn down by him, just because he was now wearing them and had previously worn them. There were a number of possibilities here, as always. One that immediately came to his mind, as the tips of his fingers traced the bottom of that tight, worn trouser pocket, was that they had mainly been worn (in both senses) by someone else or, indeed, a number of people, before they had come into his possession by whatever means, unspecified. The reason that he was sure, initially, that this was the case was the fact that he had acquired them from what is known as a second-hand shop or store. The second-hand here referred, he thought, to the secondary users of the item (which included items of clothing), with the first hand belonging to the initial owner. That was not to say that the hand (and it was never specified which was meant – left or right) of the initial owner of the item was the first hand to have touched the item. That would clearly be ludicrous. The item would have to have been made somewhere, presumably, or, at least would have to have been handled by humans if not by other apes during the process of its finding itself on the back, or in this specific case, encompassing the legs, buttocks and genital area (plus part of the hips and stomach area) of our intrepid investigator who, remember, was investigating the disappearance of his colleague, Marguerite, last seen on the trail of Harold Absalon, the Mayor's transport advisor, whose disappearance Marguerite had been investigating prior to his own disappearance. It is highly unlikely, then, that even if an animal like a sheep or cow simply shed its wool (in the former case) or skin (in both cases) that this would be shed in a form that could readily be worn by human beings, let alone by other apes, without, that is, some form of higher simian intervention. There was a possibility, granted, of genetic modification to the animals in question, immoral though our investigator thought this to be, designed to ensure that, once a year, or more regularly, they would shed their wool (in the case of sheep) in a form that could readily be used (as gloves, bobble hats, jumpers, pullovers) by human beings to cover all or part of their anatomy without further simian intervention. The case of being able to cover the whole anatomy of one human would be particularly challenging where the item was shed and then donned – he thought first of the elasticated nature of the wetsuit that deep (and more shallow) sea divers wore whilst they were diving, immediately prior to diving and immediately after diving, plus, perhaps, at other times, such as when they were demonstrating to others how to don such an outfit, that is, in the teaching sphere, if they were involved in such a sphere, and perhaps when going to a fancy dress party with an underwater theme, although it would surely be terribly hot to wear such an outfit, especially if dancing were involved, unless, of course, the theme encompassed actually being underwater – perhaps it was a party hosted by a rich benefactor such as a member of Richard Knox's[3] family (or someone who was simply rich but wasn't a benefactor) and involved time in the swimming pool of their mansion or condominium. However, in the latter case he was satisfied that this would be covered by the initial category of actual diving or the precursor or preamble to such an activity. It was, then, first, the elasticated nature of the wet- (and let us not forget the dry-) suit that he felt would not particularly lend itself to genetic modification in sheep, cows – in short, in any animal whatsoever. The reason he thought this was unlikely he would come back to in due course. Firstly, though, he couldn't help noticing that he had moved across an issue that may confuse lesser mortals than himself – that is people with lesser intellectual and imaginative capacity than he was capable of – indeed capable of but also demonstrating in this speculative outpouring. It was this: in using the terms wet- and drysuit he wanted to ensure that this was not taken in any way to relate to business suits. Of course the fact of wearing a wetsuit (or its dry equivalent, if the drysuit can be referred to in that way) did not preclude one from doing business. In fact, even when someone was wearing a wetsuit it would not preclude them from doing business, at least not in all environments that one could think of. Consider, for example, the following scenario: a dive instructor wishing to buy a dive shop

3 My misjudgment came on one of those rare social occasions attended by both Knox and myself. I would not, of course, have brought Isobel with me on that or any other such occasion. I hoped that, over time, my relationship with the wife of their former colleague would normalise within the project office; even if some may never condone it, I hoped that all, with time, would come to accept it.

from its current owner and, having just returned from a dive, she encounters the current owner as he is walking along the beach, or along the line of shops which contains the shop in which he has a business interest. There is nothing to stop her, in this scenario, to our investigator's mind, from engaging in business with the current owner just because she was wearing a wetsuit; in fact, her sporting of a wetsuit may help her in her business interest – it may demonstrate to the current owner of the dive shop, whether it needed demonstrating or not, that the potential purchaser has an interest in diving, at least to the extent that she was willing to wear a wetsuit (that would be the only evidence that the vendor would have of the potential purchaser's interest (in diving, that is), unless, of course, he had embarked on the diving trip that the potential purchaser had just returned from and seen the potential purchaser actually diving, or had previously been on a diving trip with the potential purchaser). But that is a very different situation, note, from the banker in the city going to a business meeting in the city in a wet- or even drysuit (assuming the latter's specifically nautical connotations are taken as read, 'taken as read' being *the* form of words that our investigator perhaps fears most of any form of words that he can think of). In that situation he was sure that it would *not* be possible to do business, even if all of the other people in the business meeting knew that the man or woman in a wet- or drysuit before them had an interest in diving; indeed, even if they knew that s/he had a business interest in diving; indeed, even if the meeting was about the purchase of the dive shop which has been so clearly elaborated upon in the scenario previously alluded to – that is the city banker in question and the potential purchaser of the dive shop were one and the same person (male or female or indeterminate); none of this would make it possible for the city banker/potential purchaser to do real business in the city in a wet- or drysuit as opposed to the conventional uniform of conventional business in the city, which is, of course, the business suit.

In fact it is difficult to imagine any business being conducted in a city where any rubber item of clothing is being worn by any of the parties to that business. At least, to the extent that items of rubber clothing are *visibly* being worn by the parties to a business meeting he felt that doing business would become increasingly difficult. In other words, to express it more clearly, the ineffectiveness of a business meeting *qua* business meeting was directly proportional to the surface area of visible rubber clothing being worn at that meeting. He wanted, furthermore, to ensure that one didn't go away with the thought that this was the only factor in the effectiveness of business meetings – there were many others. Indeed, he now realised (in fact, this thought had dawned on him as the previous thought was unfolding, but he had not been able to think this current thought whilst the previous thought was still unfolding for fear (albeit unconscious) of impeding the previous thought from unfolding in full) (but now the current thought, in expressing this 'bridging thought' if one can express it in that way, has been lost, so the unconscious care that he had lavished on the initial thought is somewhat undercut by the loss of the current thought, as it was previously known but which should now be known as the next thought, or nascent thought, should it reappear in nascent form in his mind, which he hopes it does, to distinguish it, that is, from the current thought (previously known as the 'bridging thought', which, in taking so long to unfold has taken over from the previously current thought in all-including-name) that (ah! it's there again!) even if the rubber clothing in question is not visible (which is not to say that it is *in*visible, just to say that it is not visible to the meeting attendees – it is underneath other items of (non-rubber) clothing, say, or underneath the meeting room table) that does not mean that its ability to undermine the conduction of effective business is diminished. In fact, he thought, it may impede more in its invisibility (as defined above) than in its visibility, depending on the item of rubber clothing in question. Granted, the wearing of a gimp suit on full display would stop any business meeting in its tracks – that much is clear. But consider, for a moment, the difference between donning a pair of rubber underpants versus the donning of a rubber belt at the meeting in question. It may be that the other attendees at the meeting do not even notice the rubber belt and that the donner of said belt forgets he or she is wearing it. Then business can be conducted without any impediment, at least without any impediment arising due to the presence of the rubber belt in the meeting. Compare this with the discomfort probably being felt by the wearer of rubber underpants on, say, a particularly warm summer's day in a meeting room without air conditioning. Would you not say, he wondered, as he discovered that the key to the padlock was not, in fact, contained within that right-hand trouser pocket, that the effect on the psyche of such discomfort on the effectiveness of their performance at the meeting, and therefore on the business of which they were a part, would be greater than the more visible item of clothing, namely the belt? Satisfied that this rhetorical question brought this particular diversion to a satisfactory closure, he felt that he really must bring his reflections back to the point at hand, which was what exactly?

It was this: that it was unlikely that a domesticated animal could produce an item of clothing having rubber-like properties or a zip, buttons, Velcro or other means of fastening. On this basis he thought that it was highly unlikely that a single item of fur, wool, leather, skin of another sort, or any other shedding from an animal, domesticated or otherwise, could perform the task of completely covering the human body, that is to say the body of a typical human subject, if there were such a thing i.e. a typical human subject. But, in thinking this, he suddenly realised that he had been thinking about the size of the typical domestic or livestock animal compared to the size of the typical human subject, and that he'd also had in his mind the idea that the item of clothing would need to be tight fitting in the way that many modern items of clothes are (including, of course, his worn, in all senses of the word, trousers): for example following the lines (not straight of course) of the legs, arms, breasts, backside or other areas of the body. This did not need to be the case. If one were to imagine a smaller human subject and a larger non-domesticated or non-livestock animal such as a bear, then one could imagine that the skin of the latter could completely cover the body of the former even without the intervention of genetic modification. Perhaps the bear had died of natural causes and then its innards had been devoured by hyenas followed by vultures, both of which species got a bad press to his mind – they fulfilled a useful function, he thought, at the very least in the example that was currently unfolding in his mind (and in this case he wasn't conscious of any queue of thoughts, as previously), leaving just skin and fur. It was quite possible to think, he thought, of a smaller human being with the ability to climb into that skin, a skin, note, that would completely cover his body. It is possible to imagine, also, that human subject walking back to the campsite inside that skin to scare his fellow campers; but that is beside the point. The point is this, in the current scenario it can truly be said that the item of clothing, if one can call it that, is truly 'first-hand' and if that person had simply donned the bearskin and walked to our investigator and handed it, one handed, to him, and that the latter had received it, one handed, then it could truly be said to be a second-hand item of clothing. It was *only* in a scenario such as the one that he had outlined that the purist can be satisfied that a second-hand item of clothing is *literally* second-hand. All other references to second-hand clothing are mere echoes of this ideal situation. Here (that is, in the impure case) second-hand is a metaphor, a short hand way of encapsulating the situation (and note that short- and second-hands refer not to the same specific hand; also note that first-hand knowledge and first-hand clothing[4] refer (mostly) to quite different situations that are not to be confused).

Satisfied that he had explored this area with a sufficient degree of thoroughness, and with his right hand still as it were ensconced within his right-hand trouser pocket, he used his gloved left hand to place his right-hand glove in his left-hand jacket pocket as a precursor, he hoped, to retrieving the keys from his left-hand trouser pocket and continuing his investigation into the disappearance of his colleague, Marguerite, last seen on the trail of Harold Absalon, the Mayor's transport advisor, who had been missing.

---

4 This, though, was at the stage where, as far as I knew, no-one knew. So it was with great alarm that, as I was standing my round – something that Harold Absalon had always been known for and which, for that reason, it behove me to do – the picture that I kept in my wallet of her wearing that favourite old sun hat next to the lake fell right at Knox's feet.

6

WHY, HE NOW wondered in frustration, had he not instigated the search for the keys prior to arriving at the gate, particularly given that he now had pursuers bearing down upon him from left and right? Why, particularly given, we hope, his extensive experience in the field, had he not initiated the usual search prior to the retrieval of the keys in question – namely the patting of pockets that his uniformed colleagues were so familiar with perpetrating on others? This he could have initiated on himself prior to his arrival there to the extent that he would at least have known if he had the keys in his possession (and he strongly suspected that he did) and, further, would have been able to locate in which pocket the keys in question resided: right- or left-hand trouser pocket, to give just the main candidates? Certainly, now that he was in this position he was not going to wait until he had fully withdrawn the glove from his left hand before checking whether the keys were contained in the equivalent trouser pocket. Instead, having removed his gloved left hand from his left-hand jacket pocket, he started pulling on the middle finger of that glove with his teeth whilst simultaneously starting to withdraw his right hand from his right-hand trouser pocket with the intention that this hand would lend assistance by approaching that left-hand trouser pocket from the exterior, so as to initiate what's known as a frisk, something that his uniformed colleagues would have had the pleasure of performing on many more occasions than himself.

Typically perpetrated on another – and particularly, unfortunately (to his mind), on another of the same sex – the frisk involved patting, in particular, but also a little bit of rubbing and squeezing, with the aim of trying to locate, as he himself would shortly be doing with his right hand, items that were either forbidden under certain circumstances or which had been lost and were in the process of being searched for. There were a number of paradigmatic locations for the frisk: the police station or other place of incarceration being one, the airport being another. In the case of the latter, the reason for the frisk related but was not limited to metallic objects that may advertently or inadvertently cause harm to others either directly or through piercing the fabric of the aircraft, particularly when that aircraft was airborne, as it's known, and particularly through the use of explosive materials which it was also the purpose of the frisk to locate.

The officer in question would initiate the frisk by asking you to spread your legs and put your arms in the air, and he would ask you to do this in one or more of a number of ways, the primary one, given the language barrier that could often exist between agents and clients, to call them that, at international airports, being the mime, which is to say the officer in question would mime the actions of putting the arms in the air and spreading the legs him- or herself as a way of indicating to the client (and in the case where they suspected that the client had some contraband of some sort – a blade or other dangerous or potentially dangerous metallic object, narcotics or even just liquids – they would refer to that person as 'the suspect' although not necessarily to their face) what they wanted them to do. This mime might, in fact, just include the initial phase of the posture requested by the agent of the client/suspect:

that of raising the arms, and this raising of the arms was, of course, a different raising of the arms to that requested – or demanded, often, for reasons that will become obvious – in the situation where firearms (not to be confused) were involved or potentially involved. There the requirement was to raise the arms and, by extension, the hands as high as possible, the purpose being to raise them to an altitude that was as distant as possible from the location or potential location of the firearm, which was typically in a holster, on a belt designed for the purpose of holding that holster, at, or hanging down from, the hip, or, for those working undercover, whether cops or robbers, as it were, in a holster concealed, by means of straps over the shoulder(s), inside one's shirt or blouse.[5] There, then, the request would be to raise one's hands – and the formulation, classically, was to 'put your hands up' – rather than to raise one's arms. Often the apprehending or arresting officer would, from behind (after the frisk, note, had perhaps been undertaken by a colleague from the front) carefully or roughly, depending on a number of factors that our investigator decided not to go into at that moment given the pressing nature of the activities he was engaged in, pull the suspect's arms down one by one, often by the wrist, so as to handcuff them, with the handcuffs also being attached one by one, which is to say that he would pull one of the suspect's arms down, from the back, as it were, generally respecting the anatomical constraints of that arm as he or she did so, then they would cuff that hand, or rather

5   His expression changed as soon as he saw her. I had not believed, until then, that one could fall for someone just from seeing a picture of them. But that is what I thought I witnessed on that occasion in that public bar around the corner from the project office. It was only a small photograph, but one in which certainly her figure was outlined to pleasing effect. And she wore that mysterious, seductive smile that one saw, from time to time, never quite knowing what to make of it.

that wrist, before bringing the next and, one hopes, final arm down in a similar although symmetrical fashion, and cuffing that hand/wrist – making sure to cuff it to the other one, previously cuffed, as a means of restraining the suspect from using their arms, with the word 'arms' in this instance actually being quite broadly defined.

The request to raise one's arms prior to the frisk was different, then, to that of putting your hands up, he realised, as he started to pull, now, on the *index* finger of his left-hand glove with his teeth whilst continuing to withdraw his right hand from his right-hand trouser pocket, with the key difference relating, he thought, to ensuring that even the shortest officer (and there were, in his day, minimum height requirements for officers, if not for private detectives) would be able to reach the full extent of the arms during the frisk whereas there was no real requirement for this in the case of putting one's hands up given that, in any case, one would hopefully be at some distance from the suspect in that situation and the intention was for them to put as much distance as possible between hands and firearm or potential firearm rather than being able to reach the full extent of the arms to complete the frisk. The key difference, then, he now realised as, travelling diagonally, given that it was moving down to the base of the opposite pocket, his right hand, having released itself from the constraints of the right-hand trouser pocket, passed towards his genital area (an area with which it had hitherto been in contact internally and secretly), en route to the left-hand trouser pocket – the external portion thereof – was that in one situation, one suspected (or, in some cases strongly suspected or simply knew, through observation) that the person in question had a firearm or firearms and it was for this reason that one need not necessarily frisk them, at least not until they had put their hands in the air, whereas in the other situation one simply needed, by a process of the elimination of evidence on a massive scale, to rule out the presence, hidden about that person, of firearms or other metallic objects of a dangerous or potentially dangerous nature.

In demonstrating, then, through a momentary mime, given the linguistic constraints that were often attendant upon such interactions at international airports, the officer in question would typically indicate that the arms should be put up, and extended, at an angle of roughly one-hundred-and-thirty-five degrees, whereas in the situation where one requests or demands that the suspect put their hands up then this would typically be understood to represent an angle of one-hundred-and-eighty degrees, the reference point for both of these arm positions being, of course, the remainder of the body when viewed from the front or rear, given that these were typically the locations from which the frisk would be undertaken by the investigating officer. The one-hundred-and-eighty degree angle was the most appropriate in the situation, then, where one suspected that the subject, to call them that now, was in possession of one or more firearms, to prevent them from accessing those firearms at speed; in other words, the one-hundred-and-eighty degree angle implied, to those with a modicum of trigonomic understanding, the placement of the hands in question at the greatest distance from the pockets/holsters containing or potentially containing the firearm(s) in question such that, were the subject to attempt to access that firearm or those firearms at speed, as a means of initiating a shootout, as it's known, which is to say the use of those firearms to facilitate their escape, then the officers in question would have given themselves the best chance of preventing the subject from accessing their firearm(s), given its or their distance from the subject's arms and, more specifically, hands, particularly as they would presumably already be pointing their own firearms at the suspect in question as a means of deterrent and restraint. This contrasts, to summarise, with the situation in which the investigating officer does not suspect that the subject has hidden about their person a firearm or firearms but wishes, is requested or is required from a legal standpoint, to frisk that person to rule out the possibility of same. Here, then, whilst it is prudent for the arms to be at some distance from the likely locations for concealing blades and firearms (as well as other forbidden items, such as narcotics or even just liquids) it is also for the arms in question not to be so distant as to make frisking them uncomfortable or impossible for those officers who were short in relation to the subject in question. It was for this reason, he thought, as his right hand passed his left testicle en route to the left-hand trouser pocket and he started pulling on the *ring* finger of his left-hand glove with his teeth, that this more acute (although still, of course, obtuse in absolute terms) angle of one-hundred-and-thirty-five degrees was adopted or requested for this purpose, which is to say for the purpose of the frisk.

The officer conducting the frisk would not typically mime the full extent of this one-hundred-and-thirty-five degree arm-angle given that it was so well represented in the cinema; nor would they even begin to mime the spreading, as it were, of the legs, which, note, did occur at an acute angle, with this angle being that subtended between the legs rather than to the subject's centre line. The angle, given the geometry, that the arms made with each other was, of course, forty-five degrees; he suspected that the angle between the legs would be more like thirty or thirty-five, for those who want a complete and accurate record of this procedure. It would, he thought, be taken as read, as it were, that the legs should be spread following the officer's indicative mime of the arm-spread. No mime was employed in the situation where the officer in question was requesting or demanding that the subject put their hands up – for what he hoped were, by now, obvious reasons.

7

A S HIS RIGHT hand made contact with the exterior of
his left-hand trouser pocket – without locating the key(s)
therein – he realised that there were also rear pockets, which is
to say that, as well as there being front trouser pockets – left
and right – and jacket pockets – left and right – there were,
of course, often, rear trouser pockets – left and right; he felt
surprised and ashamed that he had not set this out previously,
extending, as it did, by a factor of a half, the potential area of
his search. Should he be sending a hand or hands around also
to those pockets, just as, when casing a joint, as it's known,
one would send officers around to the rear so that, were the
inhabitants to flee, a flight, of course, brought about by the
entry through the front, and often with force, of investigating
officers, then those fleeing in that way could be apprehended by those officers who had gone around the back in this
way. Similarly, where drugs, say, were involved (and he had no
reason to suspect that they were in the current case) then one
might also even have to cover the drains (which is not to say
that one would literally cover them, with a wo/manhole, but,
in fact would uncover such wo/manholes) so that, similarly,
one could apprehend, by sticking one's rubber-gloved hand in
at the moment of the toilet flush, typically – the contraband
substances in this instance rather than persons in the process
of committing an offence, as it would no doubt be put down
in court.

He couldn't help noticing, as he refrained, in fact, from diverting either/both of his hands around to the rear of his trousers, to the single, in fact, pocket – buttoned, and to the right-hand side from his perspective (and from ours, given the fact that we are following in his footsteps, somehow, and, in so doing, facing, presumably, in the same, or a similar, direction to him), that references to going round the back as well as uncovering wo/manhole covers so as to stem the flow of contraband had the potential to take his investigation in a direction that he didn't want it to go in, which is to say in a direction involving the most basic of bodily functions: defecating and urinating in particular. It's not that he was squeamish about these things. Just because we have not seen him engaging in them does not, of course, mean that he does not regularly do so. There was plentiful time within which he could (although given the nature, urgency and continuity of his current investigation he thought it unlikely, in the current case, that he would have used the chapter breaks to avail himself of nearby facilities: makeshift, in the low-budget case where he had no back-up crew; mobile if he had, with the level of comfort and luxury therein no doubt dependent on his popularity or even notoriety as an investigator).

It was not, then, that he was avoiding these allusions through unfamiliarity. It was imperative, in fact, that, before each investigation, or rather, before each phase of each investigation, he use the available facilities so as to avoid an embarrassing interlude at a critical juncture: the moment of an arrest, say, or the gathering of a key piece of evidence during surveillance, or, as in the current case, the moment of entry into a property that could prove central to that investigation; an interlude, to spell it out, where he would have to go off, to find the little room set aside for the purpose and, therein, urinate and/or defecate (or, rather, urinate or urinate and defecate, given the difficulty, in his experience, of undertaking the latter without simultaneously although not necessarily continuously engaging in the former), regardless of how the chapter breaks fell.

The reason, then, that he refrained in this way from diverting one or both of his hands to the rear of his pants, to use that terminology now, related to the fact that he was concerned that dwelling upon such features might be off-putting to the more squeamish of those following in his footsteps, even though he knew that being able to deal with bodily waste – of whatever kind – was part (and, he tried, and failed, to refrain from adding, parcel) of any investigative career, particularly, to his mind, in its early stages and, secondly, and most importantly, to the fact that he was certain that the keys in question, or any keys, were not contained in that rear-most pocket given that: his posterior, to use that delicate term for the more delicate of his subordinates, had, quite recently, been in direct contact with a seat; that anything metallic and perhaps even sharp, such as a key, or a bunch of keys on a key ring enclosed within such a rear pocket, whether to the left or to the right (from his and our perspective, as before) would as it were have intervened between him (and, more specifically, his backside – left or right cheek – to use those somewhat more direct terms) and the seat; he would have noticed the (probably painful) physical sensations of this intervention and would have retained the memory of such recent sensations to be used in evidence when, as in the current scenario, he was looking for the key or keys that would literally unlock the door to the indescriptive townhouse before him that he took to be so central to his investigation into the disappearance of his colleague Marguerite, last seen

35

on the trail of Harold Absalon, the Mayor's transport advisor; and he had no such memory of such sensations; on this basis, he concluded that the keys to the townhouse were not, in fact, contained in the rear pocket of his trousers, which was the reason why he refrained from referring to going around the back, with its connotations of defecation, preferring, instead, to refer to the front portion of this area of his trousers, with its implication of the sexual, rather than a urinary or excretory function, which, in turn, would point, sometimes quite literally, to the sexual frisson that existed between himself and the wife of the transport advisor,[6] who had, in turn, been on the trail of Marguerite, his investigative colleague, prior to his disappearance, hoping that, just as with the more squeamish amongst us, this diversion to, and through, the most basic of human functions (which ordinarily must be hidden away in rooms that were often quite small and which were almost always, in his experience, gender-specific) had not put her off him, thereby jeopardising the potential for them to engage in that other basic human (and non-human) function – one that, similarly, took place in private rooms, although generally rooms of a somewhat larger size, although sometimes (and there was a whole sexual industry here), of course, in cubicles, but which readers, such as ourselves, were much happier to read about to the extent that it was quite difficult, now, to write about that latter intimate physical activity with any hope of originality.

6 Knox was suave, attractive – one never saw any cracks in his charming façade (although we all knew how decisive and unsentimental he could be). This, then, was the only moment I had seen him momentarily surprised.

8

H E STARTED NOW to bring his left foot up to accompany his right on the step that protruded from beneath the gate leading to the area in front of the townhouse in question. What he meant to say by this, as, elongating the ring finger of his left-hand glove, he finally removed that glove from his left hand whilst simultaneously locating with his right hand the keys in the far corner of his left-hand trouser pocket, was that, leaning forwards slightly and straightening his right leg, he had bent his left knee and foot such that, whilst the ball, as it's known, and the toes of that foot remained on the ground, which is to say at local ground level rather than at the level of the step that protruded from beneath the gate leading to the area in front of the townhouse in question, he had raised the heel of his left foot as a precursor to raising the remaining part of that foot to a level at which it could subsequently be moved forwards and placed alongside, or thereabouts, the right foot on the step that protruded from beneath the gate leading to the area in front of the townhouse in question. In other words he wished to elevate the lowest part of that foot, which is to say the left, to a height that was no less (and ideally more) than the height of the step that protruded (and, as far as we know, continues to protrude) from underneath the gate to the area in front of the townhouse in question so that, after he had moved that foot forwards, which is to say in the direction that he was facing, as it's known, then it would be possible to place (or in the case where the elevation of the lowest part of that foot was *equal* to the height of the step in question, slide) the foot into position alongside his other foot, which is to say his right foot.

Why this requirement, he wondered, as his heel continued to elevate almost to the point where the ball of his foot also started to elevate, to place the left foot alongside, rather than in advance of, the right? Granted that there was a gate in front of both feet, which is to say in front of him as a whole, and it might be that it was this that constrained the potential forward motion of both feet; he was, after all, even as he straightened the right and bent the left leg further so as to facilitate the passage of the left foot, as before, from local ground level to the relative elevation of the step protruding from beneath the gate leading to the area in front of the townhouse in question, simultaneously reaching downwards, now, with his left hand towards his left-hand front trouser pocket (and, given that there was no left-hand rear trouser pocket, as has been established, the use of the qualifier 'front' is surely superfluous in this instance) so as to be able to retrieve the keys to the padlock securing the gate to the area railings in front of the townhouse in question to gain access to that area – for himself if not for others – whilst reaching upwards with his right hand towards the glove that was dangling from his mouth.

Was it, then, simply the case, he wondered, as his toes left the tarmac, concrete or other material that comprised the local, presumably publically owned ground level of the pavement or sidewalk en route to the brick, concrete or stone of the presumably privately owned (by Richard Knox, remember) relative elevation of the step that protruded, and perhaps continues to protrude, in the manner previously described, which is to say, from beneath the gate leading to the area in front of the townhouse in question, that there was only sufficient space for his feet to be located side-by-side, which is to say, for his feet to be located next to each other on that step, with his left foot on the left-hand side (he would come back to this) and his right to its right, on his right-hand side (as before)? In still other words, was the step that protruded and perhaps continues to protrude from beneath the gate leading to the area in front of the townhouse in question of a similar depth, if that is the correct way in which to specify the dimension in question, as the size of his feet (assuming, for now, that his feet were of a similar size to each other) such that, were he to place his left foot onto that step that he would *have* to place it next to the right foot?

Yes and no, was his response to the question that he had posed himself and which, as his left foot commenced its descent towards that step, it (this foot) having elevated itself to a height slightly in excess, in fact, of that of the step in question as a means of avoiding having to slide forward across that step (this in the situation, remember, where the lowest part of that foot equalled, rather than exceeded, the height of the step in question), he continued to ponder. And the reason he responded in this somewhat ambiguous way to the question he had set himself, as he continued to lean forward, notice, with the still straightening right side of the body, whilst the left side, as it were, caught up, was that, as always, it depended on one's perspective. He could, he thought, confirm for us that the depth of the step more or less matched the long dimension of each of his feet, such that, when the left foot attained the step in question it must, of necessity, locate itself alongside (and to the left of) the right foot; there was, on this basis, quite simply nowhere else for it to go. But in another sense the depth of the step was much greater than this, which is to say, much greater than the distance from its edge to the nearest plane of the gate leading to the area in front of the townhouse in question (leaving aside the possibility of there being a gap underneath that gate of sufficient height for a fraction (in length) of one or more of his feet to occupy, thereby effectively extending the depth in question of the step in question). And the reason it was much greater was that it extended, in fact, from its edge all the way across the area in front of the townhouse to the steps leading up to the front door of the townhouse itself; in other words, this step that protruded from beneath the gate leading to that area was by far the deepest (or perhaps, now, he should say the longest) of the steps leading up to that front door. Granted that, as has long been established, there was a gate barring, as it were, his entry to that area and it was this that was constraining his pedicural room for manoeuvre; yet – and this was a further point that mediated or transcended the simplistic binary opposition between the similarity or difference in size of the foot, or feet, and the step in question – given that that gate was secured with a chain and padlock, there would be some flex in the crucial dimension in question, which is to say the depth (or perhaps length) of that first step i.e. the step that protruded, to use that shorthand, meaning that he would, he thought, be able to open the gate fractionally without unlocking the padlock securing it, as a mere precursor, of course, to unlocking that padlock, entering the area, and continuing his exhaustive investigation into the disappearance of his senior investigative colleague, Marguerite, who was last seen on the trail of Harold Absalon, the Mayor's transport advisor, who, previously, had gone, and then subsequently had been, missing.

9

T HERE WAS, IN fact, an opportunity for one or more
of his feet to protrude beneath the gate leading to the
area in front of the townhouse, just as the step that those feet
were placed upon protruded beneath the gate leading to the
area in front of the townhouse. In other words, were he to
want or require, for the purposes of his investigation, rather
than on a whim, to place one or more of his feet in a position
such that it - or they - were to protrude beneath the gate
leading to the area in front of the townhouse, just as the step
that that very foot - or those very feet - was, or were, placed
upon, protruded beneath the gate leading to the area in front
of the townhouse then there was an opportunity for him to do
so. And the reason that there was an opportunity for him to
place one or more of his feet in the position described, which
is to say in a position where it - or they - protruded beneath
the gate leading to the area in front of the townhouse, just as
the step upon which they were placed protruded beneath that
gate, related to the fact that the position of the gate was such
that there was a gap beneath it, a gap, in fact, between the step
that protruded from underneath the gate leading to the area in
front of the townhouse and the gate itself, a gap, moreover, of
sufficient horizontal and vertical dimension to accommodate
a foot, or feet, were this, or these, to be placed within that gap,
such that this item or these items, were it or they to be placed
in a sufficiently advanced position within that space between

protuberant step and elevated gate, could be said to protrude beneath the gate in question whilst being placed on that step which also, but in a different way, protruded beneath the same gate.

Before returning to specify, more precisely, a maximum number of feet that could be placed within this area, he wished, first, as he took his left-hand glove from his mouth with his right hand, to adumbrate how the manner in which his foot or feet, were he to place it or them in the appropriate location (which is to say in a location between the step that protruded beneath the gate leading to the area in front of the townhouse and the gate itself, in a sufficiently advanced position such that that foot, or those feet, extended beyond the vertical, two-dimensional plane formed by the side of the gate facing the townhouse in question), would differ in their protrusion from the manner in which the step that protruded beneath the gate to the townhouse in question protruded from beneath that gate. And the primary way in which his foot or feet would differ in their protrusion from that of the step upon which they were currently placed, were they to be placed in a more advanced position underneath the gate leading to the area in front of the townhouse in question such that they protruded beneath that gate, would be one of direction: the step that protruded beneath that gate protruded in our direction, which is to say it protruded towards those of us following, in whatever way on-goingly mysterious to him, in his footsteps whereas, those very footsteps, were they singly or doubly (but, he hoped, always singularly) to continue towards the area in front of the townhouse prior to him opening the gate barring him, as it were, from that area, then they would, in all likelihood, for a time, at least, protrude beneath that gate, but in the opposite direction to that of the step that protruded beneath the same gate. It was this, then, quite simply, that was the primary difference in protrusion between the step and his foot or feet, which is to say, between the actual protrusion of the step from beneath the gate to the area in front of the townhouse in question and the potential protrusion of his foot or feet beneath that same gate, which is to say the gate that he was facing, and, by extension, that we are facing, in the opposite direction from that in which the step that protruded beneath the gate was or is facing (and note that there was also a gate to the right of the area in front of the townhouse that led to the steps leading down to the basement area, the top step of which protruded beneath *that* gate, and in a still different direction, which is to say to the right from his (and from our) perspective).

And the only point he wished to clarify in terms of the quantity of the feet (and he would say nothing about their quality, given the amount of painstaking legwork he had been engaged in in attempting to unearth the circumstances of the disappearance of his esteemed investigative colleague, Marguerite, who was last seen on the trail of Harold Absalon, the Mayor's transport advisor, who had been missing) in relation to the roughly rectangular space afforded them by the area bounded by: the bottom of the gate; the two gateposts, left and right; and the step that protruded beneath that gate, was that they should total a maximum of two and, in the case where no protrusion occurred (which is to say, no protrusion of foot or feet, rather than of step, under gate) a minimum of zero, and that the number of feet, in the situation where one or more of them did, in fact, protrude from underneath the gate to the area in front of the townhouse in question, should consist of a whole number, otherwise one would have to bring the toes into play, such that one would say that one or more of the toes protruded in the manner described, and he wished to avoid this, for some reason.

10

WHY, GIVEN THE foregoing, did he refrain, then, from placing one or more (as before) of his feet beneath the gate, opting to lean towards it instead? Why, in other words, did he not move even closer to the gate, in the manner described, so as to make the leaning towards it superfluous? The reason that he hadn't placed one or more of his feet in the position described was that he had noticed that there was something lying on the floor beneath the gate. Essentially, then, by refraining from placing one or more (as before) of his feet in this location, he was momentarily preserving the scene so as to be able to examine this piece of evidence subsequently. Why, though, did he not examine the object immediately, that is before continuing to move towards retrieving the keys from his left-hand trouser pocket with his left hand whilst his right hand moved towards placing his left-hand glove in his left-hand jacket pocket (note)? Why, in other words, had he not diverted his right hand to the task of retrieving this object rather than to depositing his left-hand glove in his left-hand jacket pocket? Why was his left hand still moving towards his left-hand trouser pocket so as to retrieve the keys to enable him to unlock the padlock securing the gate leading to the area in front of the townhouse, rather than moving towards the item on the ground in front of him with the assistance, perhaps, of a crouching or squatting posture, as a means of picking up and examining said item? The rationale for the lean, compared to the crouch, squat or bend, was that, were he to pause momentarily to pick up the object, then he would be apprehended by his pursuers. That, in short, was why he continued with his current mission sub-objectives of depositing the glove and retrieving the keys as a means of gaining such access, rather than picking up what could prove to be a crucial piece of evidence, crucial, that is, to his investigation into the circumstances surrounding the disappearance of his colleague Marguerite, who was last seen in pursuit of Harold Absalon, the Mayor's transport advisor and, more specifically, the circumstances pertaining immediately prior to, and at the moment of, the disappearance(s) of said person(s).

Note that the preference for leaning, as opposed to crouching, squatting or bending, was specific to the situation as it presented itself to him at that moment. It was not, in other words, a general preference on his part. There were times when he enjoyed crouching; other times he enjoyed squatting or bending. Equally there were times when he enjoyed more than one of these actions at the same time: bending and leaning, say, or crouching and bending. And note that even though crouching and squatting could not be undertaken at the same time, really, at least not by the same person, this did not rule out his enjoying these two actions at the same time, since enjoyment did not necessarily imply any action on his part: it may be the enjoyment afforded by watching someone else crouching while he squatted, say, or vice versa, or any number of permutations thereof involving one other person or numerous other people. It was nothing, in fact, to do with enjoyment; rather it was to do with what was the appropriate furtherance of his investigation: he just knew, instinctively, that it was more appropriate to lean in the way described, rather than for him to take up one of the other bodily postures described. He knew, in other words, that it was appropriate to lean towards the gate whilst his left hand continued to move towards his left-hand trouser pocket so that it could retrieve the keys that he knew, now, were, contained therein whilst his right hand continued to move towards his left-hand *jacket* pocket so as to deposit his left-hand glove within that pocket.

This would not, of course, prevent him from examining the piece of evidence in front of him more closely as soon as he could. Nor, of course, would it prevent him from identifying the item more generally for us, as it were, as a book of matches bearing the name of the hotel from which his colleague, Marguerite, had commenced following Isobel Absalon[7] in pursuance of his investigation into the disappearance of her husband, Harold Absalon, the Mayor's transport advisor, a hotel that he knew, moreover, belonged to the family of Richard Knox. For now, though, he continued leaning towards the gate but with the added feature of twisting slightly, counter-clockwise, as an additional means of reducing the distance between: his right hand and his left-hand jacket pocket; and his left hand and his left-hand trouser pocket, as well, of course, as the contents thereof.

---

7 What was it that he saw in her that made him act in the way that he did? For now, having composed himself, he handed the photo back to me with an air of nonchalance, and simply asked, presumptuously, 'Any children?' I must have blurted out something about us trying, without success, despite myself. But he had regained his composure to the extent that my response provoked barely a flicker in his unusually smooth countenance.

11

HAVING SAID THAT the counter-clockwise twist-ing of his body was intended as an additional means of reducing the distance between: his right hand and his left-hand jacket pocket; and his left hand and his left-hand trouser pocket (as well, of course, as the contents thereof), he realised, as he continued leaning and twisting in the manner described, that this was not, in fact, his primary reason for engaging in this action. Nor did the increasing proximity of the upper reaches of his body – the head, in particular – to the gate in question, to the extent that his nose, which was the most protuberant part of that upper portion of his body, would, were this trend to continue, find itself in actual contact with the gate leading to the area in front of the townhouse, provided, of course, that it did not protrude between the bars of that gate, were the gate to be constructed in that way, or between/within any other open space that that gate, which he may, earlier on in his investigation, have identified as being of a wrought-iron construction thereby suggesting, at least to the most astute of those of us following in his footsteps, that the nose, or other, similar protuberance, may, were it to find open spaces contained within that gate of wrought-iron, interpose itself within those spaces such that it did not, in fact, come into contact with the material from which the gate to the area in front of the townhouse was constructed, had it not (his body, this was) simultaneously, or thereabouts, been twisting itself, and twisting itself, more specifically, in a counter-clockwise direction, provide the primary reason for engaging in this action. Did this counter-clockwise twisting of his body relate, he wondered, to the proximity, now, of his multifarious pursuers; which is to say, did it relate to him wanting to distance himself, albeit marginally, from them? Whilst confirming that it did, he responded, to himself, note, as well as, indirectly, to us (through some medium that must, of necessity, remain mysterious to him), by asserting that this was not the primary reason for his twisting motion either. In summary, then, just as reducing the distance between: his right hand and his left-hand jacket pocket; and his left hand and his left-hand trouser pocket (as well, of course, as the contents thereof) was a proximate but not the main reason for the twisting of his body in a counter-clockwise direction such that the head rotated further in this angular direction than the neck, which rotated further in this angular direction than the shoulders, which rotated further in this angular direction than the chest, which rotated further in this angular direction than the stomach, which rotated further in this angular direction than the hips, which rotated further in this angular direction than the genitals, which rotated further in this angular direction than the knees, which rotated further in this angular direction than the ankles, which rotated further in this angular direction than the feet (which did not, in fact, rotate at all, of course), nor, in fact, was the proximity of his nose to the gate, which is to say that the avoidance of such contact did provide a rationale for the twisting of his body in the manner described (which is to say the twisting in a counter-clockwise direction such that the head rotated further in this angular direction than the neck, which rotated further in this angular direction than the shoulders, which rotated further in this angular direction than the chest, which rotated further in this angular direction than the stomach, which rotated further in this angular direction than the hips, which rotated further in this angular direction than the genitals, which rotated further in this angular direction than the knees, which rotated further in this angular direction than the ankles, which rotated further in this angular direction than the feet (which, as before, did not, in fact, rotate at all, of course) but, as before, it was not the primary reason, just as the proximity of his multifarious pursuers was not the primary reason either. What then, given that the proximity of: his right hand to his left-hand jacket pocket; his left hand to his left-hand trouser pocket (as well, of course, as the contents thereof); his nose to the plane, and perhaps also to the material, of the gate; and his multifarious pursuers to him, had not been the determining factors in the commencement of his twisting in the manner described (and on this one, rare, occasion he spared us the details), what was that determining factor, he wondered, as, continuing to twist and, note, lean, in the manner described, his shoulder, the right, made contact with the gate leading to the area in front of the townhouse? It was, in fact, this very contact, for those still requiring such clarification, that had been the reason for him twisting and leaning in the manner described (which is to say twisting in a counter-clockwise direction such that the head rotated further in this angular direction than the neck, which rotated further in this angular direction than the shoulders, which rotated further in this angular direction than the chest, which rotated further in this angular direction than the stomach, which rotated further in this angular direction than the hips, which rotated further in this angular direction than the genitals, which rotated further in this angular direction than the knees, which rotated further in this angular direction than the ankles, which rotated further in this angular direction than the feet (which, as before, did not, in fact, rotate at all, of course). He had, in other words, rotated in this way (which is to say the twisting in a counter-clockwise direction such that the head rotated further in this angular direction than the neck, which rotated further in this angular direction than the shoulders, which rotated further in this angular direction than the chest, which rotated further in this angular direction than the stomach, which rotated further in this angular direction than the hips, which rotated further in this angular direction than the genitals, which rotated further in this angular direction than the knees, which rotated further in this angular direction than the ankles, which rotated further in this angular direction than the feet (which, as before, did not, in fact, rotate at all, of course) in order to bring about contact between the right shoulder and the gate such that the latter, which is to say the gate leading to the area in front of the townhouse would begin, at least, to open (and note that the way in which it did this was by turning, rather than twisting, on its hinges, which were, remember, to his right, such that this turning traced a *clock*wise arc when seen from above (often when seen from above), at least to the extent that the constraints of the locked chain wrapped around it allowed. It was, then, this police procedural – that of putting one's shoulder to it, as it may, or may not, be referred to in the manuals – that was the main reason he had started to twist his body whilst leaning it, at the same time, remember, as reaching: with his right hand, across his body, towards his left-hand jacket pocket; and with his left-hand towards his left-hand trouser pocket, a pocket that he knew contained a bunch of keys that would allow him not only to access the area in front of the townhouse but to enter the townhouse itself in search of the circumstances of the disappearance of his senior investigative colleague, Marguerite, who, in turn, had last been seen on the trail of Harold Absalon, the Mayor's transport advisor, who had, prior to this, been missing.

12

A ND WHAT HE found, as he continued to push the
gate open in the manner described (which, for now, he
refrained from summarising) was that, rather than becoming
fully taut, the chain that he had believed was securing the gate
to the gatepost as a means of barring entry to those, unlike
him, who had no key to the padlock securing that chain, was,
in fact, simply coiled around the gate and gatepost in a manner
that, whilst it kept the two elements of that perimeter security system momentarily together, it only did so to the extent
that, were someone, such as him, to simply uncoil it, then that
simple act would be sufficient to gain access to the area in front
of the townhouse in question. In other words, whilst giving
the appearance of securing the gate to the gatepost such that
one would need a key to unlock it, the padlock, whilst being
secured to the chain that was rapidly, now, uncoiling from
around the gate and gatepost, was not secured to that chain in
a way that would serve to prevent one from accessing the area
in front of the townhouse by traversing the gateway that was
rapidly, still, opening up through the pressure of his shoulder
against the gate that would need to open to form the gateway
to the area in front of the townhouse which he wished to move
into. There was a manner, then, in which the padlock locked
into the chain that continued to uncoil (counter-clockwise,
note) based on the pressure he continued to apply (a pressure
which he, in fact, intensified, given the success he was finding

in this propulsive strategy) such that the gate continued to open (clockwise, remember) could be locked into that chain to give at least the impression that it was securing the gate to its post (to refer to it in that fashion, now, and possibly again in the future) whilst it was not, in fact, doing so. (It could, also, of course, be locked in that way – which is to say to give the impression that it was securing the gate to its post whilst *in fact* securing the gate to its post, and in that way deterrent, in the form of appearance, would be backed up by actual security, unlike in the present instance.)

Conscious of his struggle to express, with precision, the circumstances that he found unfolding, or rather uncoiling, unravelling, before him, he decided to go back to first principles, and in the following way: in order for a padlocked chain to be used effectively to secure a gate to its post such that those without a key to that padlock would be unable to secure access to the area beyond that gate (assuming that the gate and its posts, left and right, formed part of a wider, and deeper, gate-line, as it is known, around that area, as in the current scenario) then the chain must circle around both gate and post – specifically it must circle around the gate and its post at the point where the gate would ordinarily open (the left-hand side of the gate and the left-hand gatepost in the current instance) and it must be secured in that arrangement so that it was sufficiently tight to prevent the gate opening widely enough for someone to pass under or over that chain and through the gateway that had been opened up by the slackness of the chain secured in this fashion, despite it being secured in the way described. The chain must, then, circle tightly around both post and the edge of the gate closest to that post and be secured, with the padlock, such that the padlock connected links in the chain that would maintain that circle, as well as sufficient tautness to prevent entry through the slackness to which he had previously alluded. That this wasn't the case in the current situation was evidenced, as before, by the fact that the chain continued to uncoil anti- or counter-clockwise around the left-hand gatepost as the gate continued to open in a clockwise fashion around the fulcrum of the right-hand gatepost, to the extent that the chain had nearly, now, completely uncoiled and would be left hanging, he thought, from the gate as it continued to swing open in the way so recently described.

The chain did not, of course, have to form a perfect circle – that would, he thought, be too much to ask for; what was not too much to ask for – what was, in fact, part of the rudiments of the security of such situations – was the previously referred to requirement that the circle, ellipse, oval, or other similar shape (and there would no doubt be a word for the family of such shapes that he, or we, could look up using whatever extant reference system that took his, or takes our, fancy) should be secured around both gate and post as a means of both keeping those two elements together and of demonstrating that it was keeping those two elements together, rather than in the current case where it had appeared to him, and by extension, to us, that the padlock secured to the chain would, by being so secured, prevent, through restraining the gate in the manner described, its clockwise angular movement (with the clock in question being viewed from above, even though this went against the ordinary, day-to-day, convention that clocks should be placed in locations where people such as ourselves could see them, as a means, of course, of telling the time, regardless of whether those clocks were analogue, as in the current situation, or digital). That this was not the case in the current situation

- that the chain had been secured, in circular fashion, but not in such a way as to secure the non-hinged vertical edge of the circumferential frame of the gate to the gatepost that was closest to that edge – was evidenced by the fact that the chain, now, finally swung loose from that gatepost and collided noisily with the gate to which it was attached, allowing him access, finally, to the area in front of the townhouse, without so much as needing to retrieve the key to the padlock in question, a key that we now know him to have about his person.

Why, he wondered, as he placed the glove in his left-hand jacket pocket and commenced the transition from leaning to crouching, as a precursor to retrieving the book of matches that had been located underneath the gate, had the inhabitant(s) of that house, or others who weren't inhabitants of that house, wanted to give the impression that a chain that had simply been wrapped, numerous times, around the left-hand gatepost, was, in fact, securing the non-hinged, vertical edge of the gate adjacent to that gatepost to that gatepost by means of a locked padlock? Was it that they wanted to give the impression that the townhouse was uninhabited but secured, whereas it could be that it was, in fact, inhabited and *un*secured? If so, who was it that was inhabiting this unsecured space, and why did they want to give the impression that they weren't and that it was? It was with these, and numerous other pressing questions, that he would enter the area in front of the townhouse, pursued, he was sure, by Harold Absalon, who, despite our investigator's success in opening up that area would want to do everything he could to prevent him from opening up the townhouse itself, given its centrality to the investigation into the disappearance of Marguerite, last seen, remember, on the trail of Harold Absalon, the Mayor's transport advisor, who had hitherto been missing.

13

H E WAS RELIEVED that, since the gate was unsecured, he would not have to retrieve the keys from his
left-hand trouser pocket prior to entering the area in front of
the townhouse, and the reason he was relieved related to the
fact that, in that circumstance, which is to say, him having to
retrieve the keys from his left-hand trouser pocket, he would
have run the risk, as it is known, were he to have had to retrieve
the keys prior to entering the area in front of the townhouse,
of a passer-by snatching them from his hand; he would not,
however, have been holding them out if he knew there to be a
passer-by passing him by at that moment. The reason he would
not have been holding them out under those circumstances
was that he didn't want a passer-by to snatch the keys, and
the reason that he didn't wish for that eventuality was that he
wanted to use the keys to open the front door to the townhouse, knowing, somehow, that the secret to the disappearance
of his senior colleague Marguerite, last seen on the trail of
Harold Absalon, the Mayor's transport advisor, lay therein.

The only passers-by in the vicinity at that moment remained
his multifarious pursuers and they could not properly be
classed as such as 'passers-by' for the obvious reason that they
wanted to apprehend him for peaceful or less peaceful purposes
and this apprehension, so to speak, would involve moving directly *to* him rather than passing him, let alone passing him by,
were there to be any difference, in fact, between these two latter

phrases and activities. They would make straight, or there-abouts, for him, his pursuers, he was sure of that. Another way of establishing this fact in his mind was to think to himself that to the extent that the people in his vicinity were pursuing him, then, to that extent, they would not be passers-by in relation to him.

How, though, did he know he was being pursued, he wondered, as, having successfully completed the transition from leaning to crouching, he examined, more closely, the book of matches? His reasoning was as follows: he suspected – strongly – that Marguerite had got too close to unearthing the circumstances of Harold Absalon's disappearance and that it was the proximity to these circumstances that had precipitated his disappearance. In other words, when an investigation is underway in which there is, in fact, substance to the assertion that an unlawful act had taken place, or that an unlawful act was taking place, then, at the point where those who had perpetrated that act, or who were engaged in that activity, became aware that an investigator was as it were (and literally) on their case, which is to say at the moment when that investigator's cover is blown, as it's known, a chain of association would immediately be set up in the sense of human (or, granted, in certain circumstances, canine) subjects in pursuit of one another, which, in this case, he thought, had taken the form of missing person (Harold Absalon, the Mayor's transport advisor) pursued by investigator (Marguerite) pursued by alluring, possibly dangerous, certainly unreliable and volatile female (Isobel Absalon, the wife of the missing transport advisor),[8] plus, perhaps, henchmen (and, granted, -women) intent on thwarting the investigation

8 I pondered his question afterwards. Did he know, even then, that he would have her – just on the basis of a view of her in a small, dog-eared photograph? Was that really how he operated?

for reasons relating to the circumstances surrounding the disappearance, a chain of association that, at the point where the law enforcer, to call them that, gets too close to unearthing those circumstances, would dramatically collapse, in that those who were, in turn, following him would close in, as it's known, and at speed, as a means of thwarting that investigation knowing that he was on to something, and thereby confirming to the investigator themselves, perhaps, that they were on to something although at a point where it is too late to act on this realisation, given what his pursuers would perpetrate at that moment (assuming, as before, that he wasn't able to stay at least one step ahead of them).

All he was perhaps saying was that, to the extent that Marguerite's disappearance related to the latter getting too close to the circumstances of Harold Absalon's disappearance, then, given that he, in turn, felt quite close, now, to unearthing the circumstances surrounding Marguerite's disappearance and, by extension, the circumstances surrounding the disappearance of the man Marguerite had been pursuing at the point of his disappearance, namely Harold Absalon, the Mayor's transport advisor,[9] then not only would he – Marguerite's still unnamed investigative colleague – be being pursued (despite us not having seen the start of this pursuit at the moment of his cover having been blown, which may, of course, have taken place between books – not that he could possibly have any conception of this) but that his pursuers, in turn, assuming he had not had the craft or the art to shake them off completely, would be rapidly closing in on him as a means of thwarting his investigation into the disappearance of his investigative

9   It would seem so, with this question about offspring being, to my mind, a preliminary assessment of the likely extent of the collateral damage that would be caused by his actions.

colleague and the subject that his investigative colleague had been in pursuit of at the point of the latter's disappearance, with all this perhaps being underpinned by some universal investigative law involving the interplay of attraction and re-pulsion that he would, he hoped, sketch out much more fully at his leisure, were he ever to enjoy any given the demands of his role, the assiduousness with which he pursued it and the precariousness of the situation he currently found himself in. That all this was the case was confirmed, for him, by the sound of footsteps indicative of someone (or more than one) walking towards him being heard, by him, and it was partially at least for this reason that he wished to enter, as soon as he could, the relative safety of the area in front of the townhouse if not the interior of the townhouse itself.

14

H E WAS AWARE, then, throughout these reflections, of the movements of his pursuers, who were now just a few feet away from him to his left, with Harold Absalon converging, he thought, from further away to the right. He had his back to them, as it's known, as he crouched, opening the book of matches with his right hand to examine its interior, but could adjudge their approach from the sounds of their footsteps, which he could pick out, quite distinctly, from other sounds in his vicinity. He knew that the pursuers approaching from the left were just at the point at which they could turn towards him and apprehend him - either that or they would simply pass behind him and move on a trajectory towards Harold Absalon, perhaps thereby holding up the previously missing transport advisor, not necessarily with a gun, although this couldn't be ruled out given the perilous circumstances that were unfolding. His pursuers were, then, behind and to one side of him facing in a direction at right angles to the direction in which he was facing: they were facing, in short, back up the road from whence, presumably, he had come, whereas he was facing the townhouse wherein lay the solution, he was certain, to his investigation into the disappearance of his colleague, Marguerite, last seen, as we well know, on the trail of Harold Absalon, the Mayor's transport advisor. These pursuers were walking briskly, he thought, and, if they carried on in similar vein, as it were, and upon a similar trajectory then they would very shortly pass behind him – they would, in short, move from being pursuers or potential pursuers or even accomplices, were it to emerge that a crime had been committed in relation to the disappearance of his colleague, Marguerite, to being just passers-by or even to being in the category of those who might assist him in his investigation into the disappearance of Marguerite perhaps by holding up Harold Absalon, with or without resort to a firearm, or in some other way, but not literally in the sense of holding him physically aloft. This, then, was the moment that he had come to, crouching, still, examining, now, the interior of the book of matches in his right hand, whilst his left was momentarily prevented, by the constriction in that pocket brought about by the crouch, from entering the equivalent, which is to say the left-hand trouser pocket, to withdraw – or even to contact – a bunch of keys that he knew, now, to be present, keys to a gate and a house that could prove crucial to his investigation.

It was not that he had frozen at that moment. A lesser operative might have frozen even just momentarily, breathlessly, at such a critical juncture in the investigation. He, though, was simply waiting, with the appearance of absolute nonchalance, as he noticed that only one of the matches had been used, to see, just like us, how it would turn out. Unlike us, though, in that moment he had processed the consequences of all of the conceivable outcomes of his pursuers' actions and was prepared to move to immediate implementation of one of numerous secret, still, to us, plans in response to the next minute movements of same. But none of these plans proved necessary: the pursuers who had been approaching from the left moved, at that moment, from being his potential pursuers to being passers-by or potential passers-by given that some of them were still to actually pass him by. This did not, of course, rule out game-playing by these pursuers; he was well aware that this manoeuvre on their part, as it were, could simply be a ruse to put him at his ease, to take him off his guard, as it were, so that they could then approach him from behind. He was, of course, well aware of this, and, without reducing his level of alertness, processed a number of subsidiary plans dependent on this and other eventualities on their part, plans that we, again, do not seem to have access to, either because they have not yet been declassified or simply because they were being processed at the back of his mind in a place that we, for whatever reason, cannot 'see'. At the same time he got to his feet, as it's known, with the book of matches in his right hand and the bunch of keys accessible again to his left (which is to say, within his left-hand trouser pocket, accessible to his left hand). In the next moment his pursuers had all passed behind him, thereby putting themselves in a clear category and allowing him to focus all of his energies on simply passing through the gateway and finally entering the relative safety of the area in front of the townhouse, pursued still, as far as he knew, by Harold Absalon, the Mayor's transport advisor, who had been missing.

15

T HE AREA RAILINGS enclosed, as is to be expected, the area in front of the townhouse in question, yet
they did not, in fact, separate that area from the townhouse
itself. This he realised – or understood more fully – only as he
passed into the area in question. And the way in which the area
railings enclosed the area in front of the townhouse without
excluding the townhouse itself related to the fact that, once one
had entered the area enclosed by the railings, as he had now, of
course, done, one was, in fact, free to move directly through
it, as he was doing, and into the townhouse, particularly in
the situation that he found himself in where he had a key
that would literally unlock, he thought, the front door to that
townhouse. In other words, and quite simply, the townhouse
itself acted, effectively, as the fourth and perhaps final side of
the area railings in that those railings terminated at points at
the extreme left and right of the demesne of the house and were
affixed thereon such that there was no gap between them and
the wall that formed that façade whilst simultaneously acting,
as it were, as the fourth and perhaps final side of the square
or rectangle that was the shape of the perimeter around the
area in front of the townhouse in question. He realised that
perhaps the cardinal points would explicate the point most
efficiently, but was not clear enough about the orientation of
the townhouse in space to feel confident using these, so he
put them to one side for now. Instead he relied, once again, on

the fact that, given that the whole mass of us are following in his footsteps and, as has been established previously must, for that reason, be facing in the same direction as he is (or was), then he could, without jeopardising the clarity for which he hoped, like his investigative colleague and mentor, Marguerite, he was renowned simply use the descriptors 'left', 'right', 'in front of', and 'behind', to indicate which section of the area railings (and their surrogate – the façade of the townhouse itself) he was referring to (and leaving aside the question of whether the area in front of the townhouse was – or is – big enough to accommodate all of us or whether some of the more tardy investigators amongst us would be left outside the area bounded by the area railings simply because, with so many of us potentially crowding in here, or there, following, he hoped, in his footsteps, that they – perhaps even we – would, in fact, find ourselves, some of us, excluded from that area).

The section, then, of the area railings that was behind him and (some if not all of) us contained, of course, the gate leading into that area, a gate, remember, that was open and which had not, in fact, been locked whilst giving the appearance, even to an investigator of his calibre, of having been padlocked shut as he, and we, had approached it; nevertheless, it was this potential lockability, to call it that, that enabled that section of the area railings to function in the intended fashion, which is to say, as a barrier that, when connected up effectively with other similar sections of barrier, enclosed an area and, more specifically, enclosed the area in front of the townhouse that some if not all of us would find ourselves within.

Similarly with the railings to the left and to the right of us: those to the right were connected to the section behind him (and some if not all of us) to form one corner in the

secure square or rectangular perimeter that was the area railings, although finding a precise description for that corner was
hampered, partly, by uncertainty as to our precise geo-location
within that area – even if we assume we are among the fortunate few to have found ourselves within it, a conundrum that
can, perhaps, be solved by referring to the corner formed by
the sections of the area railings that were behind us and to our
right as being diagonally opposite the corner formed by the
façade of the townhouse in front of us and the section of area
railings to our left; this would, he thought, be satisfactorily
precise, if somewhat redundant geometrically speaking; similarly, he thought, for the corner that was behind us to our left:
this was, by definition, diagonally opposite the corner formed
by the façade of the townhouse in front of us and the section
of area railings to our right. By extension, then (and he felt
pleased that he had set up the conditions for describing this,
now, adequately well, he hoped), he could say, for completeness,
that the corner formed by the intersection (was the word) of the
area railings in front of us to our right with the façade of the
townhouse proper was diagonally opposite the corner formed
by the sections of the area railings to our left and behind us,
and that the corner formed by the intersection (was still the
word) of the area railings to our left with the façade of the
townhouse proper was diagonally opposite the corner formed
by the sections of the area railings to our right and behind us;
furthermore, at the instant, which was still some way off, when
one of us passed through the dead centre of that area then that
person could say, if they wished, that: the corner formed by
the sections of area railings behind them and to their right was
diagonally behind them to their right; the corner formed by the
sections of the area railings behind them and to their left was

diagonally behind them to their left; the corner formed by the intersection of the area railings to their right with the façade of the townhouse in front of them was *diagonally* in front of them to their right; and the intersection of the area railings to their left with the façade of the townhouse in front of them was *diagonally* in front of them to their left.

It was, then, these two corners in front of us, to the left and right, that were, in fact, the end points of the area railings; at those points, quite simply, the front façade of the townhouse took over as the means of bounding the area in front of same; something similar no doubt happened at the rear of the property, assuming that there was some outside space at that rear. Satisfied that the point had been made adequately clearly, even when judged against his more than exacting standards, he terminated this illuminating interlude so as to engage, once again, more directly, with his investigation into the disappearance of his investigative colleague, Marguerite, last seen on the trail of Harold Absalon, the Mayor's transport advisor, who had been missing.

16

NOTE THAT, IF the padlock had been unlocked, he would not have needed the keys had he wished to relock it. The reason he would not have needed the keys was because the padlock was of the conventional type such that once it was unlocked, which is to say once it was open, then any fool could lock it, which is to say that any fool could close it again. Such was the conventional padlock's mechanism. In fact, it was only what was known as the 'dead lock' that didn't lend itself to this mode of operation; in the case of the dead lock any fool needed a key to both lock *and* unlock it. This was a different sort of deadness, note, to the deadness of dead matches. In fact it was so different that he thought more than once about following up this lead, as, moving through the area in front of the town-house, he slid his left hand into his left-hand trouser pocket whilst continuing to scrutinise the book of matches which he held between the thumb and index finger of his right hand. However, given the critical juncture that he had now entered upon in his investigation (etc), he felt that he must proceed with this lead; he felt, in short, that he must, as the training manuals put it, leave no stone unturned in investigating the circumstances surrounding the disappearance (etc).

The primary difference in 'deadness' between dead matches and dead locks was what? He brought in a third category to assist him: that of the dead leg. The dead leg was the closest of the examples to actual deadness, if one thinks of this term, as one traditionally does, as the opposite of aliveness. Quite simply a dead leg, or a dead arm for that matter, seemed, to its owner, so to speak, which is to say, to the person whose body it was a part of, and possibly to others observing that person, to have become momentarily lifeless; at least that person and any observers perceiving this deadness hoped, traditionally, in his view, that the lifelessness in that limb was momentary and, furthermore, brief. Leaving aside the reasons why the limb's owner wished the lifelessness of that limb to be momentary and brief, he turned his mind to what this lifelessness consisted in, as he moved purposefully through the area in front of the townhouse whilst noticing that the book of matches had scribbled, in ballpoint, inside it, a sequence of two- and three-digit numbers arranged geometrically, in a hopscotch pattern. What he came up with in this regard was that lifelessness consisted, quite simply, in a lack of animation or the potential for animation. Could this definition of lifelessness be applied, he wondered, in the case of the dead match and the dead lock as a means of teasing out the difference between them? Certainly it was clear to him that a dead match, in its inability to bring forth flame when struck against a rough surface (including, in the case of the cowboy or, in rare cases, -girl, the sole of the boot) could be defined as dead in the sense of lack of fiery animation or the potential for such animation. But in the case of the dead *lock?* Locks of whatever kind, being of a man- (or, granted, woman-) made, mechanical mien almost by definition were unanimated – indeed, were *inanimate.* They did not, then, lend themselves to being alive. There was, then, at least one difference between the dead lock and the dead match – and indeed the dead leg: the dead lock did not have an alternative 'live' disposition whereas the dead match and the dead leg did. The sense of lifelessness in the case of the dead lock was not, to restate or reformulate, in comparison to a latent potentiality for life in that type of lock, that is in the dead lock. Rather the adjective referred, he thought, to another category of lock altogether and not one, to his disappointment, that could simply be dubbed 'the live lock'. Even though this category of lock could not be labelled in this way it was still clear, he thought, which locks fell into which category, in that a lock was either dead or not, so to speak. Given that this was the case, in what sense of aliveness or liveliness does the category of lock that is not a dead lock refer? And how does that sense of aliveness or liveliness differ from that sense as applied to the leg or the match, both in their non-dead, as it were, state? Was a building taken to mimic something inert when it was in a deadlocked state and, if so, how did this inertness differ from that of the dead match or the dead leg?

He felt that the word 'deadlock' might be of some assistance in this matter, if he could only focus his mind on it rather than on the sound of his pursuer's footsteps that he thought he could hear just behind him. When talks were deadlocked it implied, to his mind, that there was no *movement* and, with that word he came, perhaps, upon the unifying feature of the dead lock, leg and match, *viz*, the *lack of movement*. Granted the movement of which the deadness signified a lack came in different guises in the three instances: in the case of the leg it might most simply be a lack of movement in the leg itself (although he realised that it was more to do with a lack of feeling in that leg, rather than a lack of movement *per se*, but he left that objection to one side for the moment); in the case of the match, the lack of movement could be taken to relate to the flickering of the flame; and in the case of the lock the lack of movement could relate to the lock itself, when deadlocked, or to movement through the door or other aperture that had been deadlocked in this way. So far, so unsatisfactory, he thought, as he tried to fathom the meaning of the geometric arrangement within the book of matches. For it was only really the dead lock itself that fully exemplified this lack of movement when in its moribund, as it were, state. At least to that extent it resembled the dead body itself; the dead match and the dead leg, given that they both lent themselves to movement could not be compared in the same way to what must be taken as the defining example of something that was dead and to which all other dead things must surely be compared. Perhaps it was to other features of the dead body that the dead match and the dead leg referred – say lack of warmth in the former case and lack of feeling in the latter? Promising though this new angle on this branch of his inquiry was, he had to bring it to an abrupt close given that a partially clad woman had appeared, momentarily, at a first-floor window of the townhouse before abruptly disappearing again, a woman, moreover, that he knew to be Isobel Absalon, the wife of Harold Absalon, the Mayor's transport advisor whose disappearance Marguerite had been investigating prior to his own disappearance.

17

T HE QUESTION NOW was whether he would be able to make it to the front door of the house before Isobel Absalon did. They would, of course, be approaching the door from different sides. That much was obvious even to the lowliest investigative recruit, he suspected. Nevertheless he spelt out, as it were, the reasons more fully, some of them at least, why he and Isobel Absalon would be approaching the front door of the house in question from different sides, as he closed the book of matches with the thumb of his right hand, before setting out why making it to his side of it first, that is, before Isobel Absalon made it to her side, was so crucial to his investigation into the disappearance of Marguerite, last seen on the trail of Harold Absalon, the Mayor's transport advisor, and colleague, or former colleague, of Richard Knox, [10] whom Harold Absalon had fallen out with prior to his own disappearance.

Firstly Isobel Absalon was inside the house whilst he was outside it. That was how things stood at that moment although, note, neither of the actual subjects of the inquiry into why those subjects would approach opposite, to express it in that way, sides of the front door to the house in question were themselves stationary. At least he suspected that Isobel Absalon was not stationary at that moment given that she had abruptly

10 Let's just say he had a reputation. Perhaps that was why I had never mentioned him to Isobel, despite the growing professional closeness between him and me.

disappeared from the window, as it were, on the upper floors
of the house in question very shortly after he had spotted her
there, which he had taken as a sign that Isobel Absalon was
on the move and more specifically was on the move towards
the front door, opposite side to him, of the house in question;
it could be that she had paused, momentarily, on seeing him,
perhaps sitting on the king-sized bed [11] behind her as a means of
what is known as collecting her thoughts – specifically, in that
case, her thoughts with regard to the presence of a detective
of his calibre in the area in front of the townhouse, and what
she was going to do in that regard knowing, as she must, the
key part that she had no doubt played in the disappearance
of his investigative colleague who, remember, was last seen,
as it were, on the trail of her husband, Harold Absalon, the
Mayor's transport advisor who had himself been missing –
not that Isobel Absalon would necessarily know that he was a
detective and, if she did, what calibre of detective he was; but
he suspected that Isobel Absalon would, before long, sense
that his presence in the area in front of the townhouse related
somehow to an investigation into her role in the disappearances
of both his colleague and her husband and would, for reasons
that he would come onto, swiftly make for the front door of
the house in question, that is, the house that she currently
occupied, which was not to say, necessarily, that this was the
house that she currently resided in – that was a different point
that he did not go into, as it is known, at that moment, so
intent was he on illustrating why he and Isobel Absalon, who
were both approaching the same front door, were, nevertheless,

11 Why did I think her unlikely to cheat on me? After all, she was, with
me, already cheating on her husband. Was it simply conceit, a sense
that, unlike Absalon, I was truly giving her what she wanted, was so
conscientiously fulfilling her every need – and not just in the bedroom?

approaching different sides of that door and were, more specifically, approaching opposite sides of that door.

Now it could be said, if the door were open and at right angles, say, to the plane of the door frame, that, in that instance, he and Isobel Absalon would both be approaching the same side of the front door in question. The front door was not open in the actual situation but he hoped that by imaginatively opening it, as it were, that this might shed light on why in the actual situation he and Isobel Absalon were almost inevitably approaching opposite sides of that door. In the case, then, where the door was open in the way described, which is to say in the way imagined by him, and assuming that the trajectory of both subjects, to call them that, was towards the doorway, that is the area that the door frame framed, then the front of the front door to the house in question, assuming that that door opened inwards, as it is known and as is traditional, would be to his left, assuming that he approached the doorway in a forward direction as, again, it is known and as is traditional, whereas the front of the front door to the house in question would be to the right of Isobel Absalon, assuming that the same parameters applied, that is the door opening inwards, which, given it is the same example as that relating to him, could reliably be taken as read, as it is known, and that she, like him, approached the doorway in a forward direction, as it is known and as is traditional, as before. He realised, as he continued to move closer to the front door in question whilst tucking the flap of the book of matches under the lip, so called, of same, that the fact that the open door would be to his left and to Isobel Absalon's right as they approached it was simply to say, albeit in a somewhat different way, that he and Isobel Absalon were approaching opposite sides of the front door to the house in question without explaining why that was the case; in other words what he had hoped would help him expedite this branch of his inquiry had ended up simply begging the question which, again, was why he and Isobel Absalon would approach, in all likelihood, given the parameters outlined, different, which is to say opposite, sides of the front door to the house in question.

One key reason why he and Isobel Absalon were approaching opposite sides of the front door to the house in question was, he now contended, that nobody could be in two or more places at the same time. He used 'nobody' instead of 'no body' advisedly since, in the latter case it was, he thought, patently obvious that it was possible for a body, as it would then be referred to, to be in two or more places at the same time. Leaving that aside for the moment, and possibly in perpetuity, he returned to his contention that nobody, which is to say no living person, nor, in fact, any dead person whose body remained intact and of a piece, as it were, could be in two or more places at once. Given the fact that he and Isobel Absalon were on opposite sides of a façade whose primary, if not its only, aperture, so to speak, was the front door, and that both subjects were alive - he was sure of this in his own case - as sure as he could be about anything - and based on having just seen Harold Absalon's wife Isobel Absalon at the window, as it is known, extrapolated to the latter's continuing existence as a living person - then to the extent that both parties, to call them that now, were converging on the same point, without either of them having crossed the façade by any other means, such as through one of the windows, whether open or closed, although, note, that in the case of crossing the threshold via a closed window a possibility opened up, so to speak, of somebody and not just some body actually being in two places at the same time, in the scenario of the body being sliced cleanly in half by the broken glass, assuming that is the substance out of which the window is made, and both halves of that body, however briefly, managing to stay alive, one on the inside and one on the outside of the house in question, then they – he and Isobel Absalon in this case – would approach that point from opposite sides. Looking at it in plan view, which is to say two-dimensionally, yields the following: Subject A on one side of a line and Subject B on the other; neither subject can be subdivided without losing their integrity, as it were; both subjects taking the shortest route to the same point on the line in question and having to navigate other objects along that route; one subject arriving at the line before the other or both arriving at the same time; assuming that neither subject, or both, have gone around either end of the line, or extending the line to infinity in both directions to prevent this from occurring; then, in converging on the same point in the line they will arrive at that point at the same or different times but on opposite sides of the line. To do it in three dimensions now, as he placed the book of matches in the upper reaches of his right-hand trouser pocket, but taking the façade and the door therein as a two-dimensional, that is, as a very flat plane, and one infinitely large, then it is simply not possible for two subjects starting on either (which is to say, one on each) side of that infinitely flat, infinitely extensive plane to arrive at the infinitely flat but finite front door in that plane – and leaving aside how one decides, now, which is the front and which is the back – it is just not possible for the subjects to arrive at the same side of that flat (in the geometrical rather than residential sense) front door and, given that there are only two sides to it given that it is infinitely flat, they must arrive, as would be the case with him and Isobel Absalon, on opposite sides of it, assuming that neither of them had found a way of crossing the façade by another means, and leaving aside any notion that there was a back door or even lower front door (which there is, or was) out of the basement of the building through which Isobel Absalon could emerge, thereby potentially meeting our investigator on the *same* side of the door in question at the same or at a somewhat different time.

Unsatisfying though he found the foregoing, he still asserted that it was at least highly likely that he and Isobel Absalon would arrive on opposite sides of the front door to the house in question and further asserted that it was imperative that he arrived at 'his' side of the door, as it were, before Isobel Absalon arrived at 'her' side of same and the reason for this was that if he didn't then Isobel Absalon would find some means of further securing the door from within such that he would find it very difficult or even impossible to open the door in question, that is the front door to the house in question, and this would make it correspondingly very difficult or impossible for him to enter the house and continue his investigations into the disappearance of his colleague, Marguerite, last seen in pursuit of Harold Absalon, the Mayor's transport advisor and husband of Isobel Absalon, an investigation, remember, that he felt sure would find a solution if not a resolution within the house in question.

Given that Isobel Absalon was inside the house, she had more means of securing the door to prevent intruders from entering, which is to say that Isobel Absalon had more means at her disposal than he had, from the outside, of securing the door to prevent extruders from exiting, not that he was interested in securing the door for this or any other reason of course. The means at Isobel Absalon's disposal included: shooting the bolts, as it is known; propping a chair under the handle, assuming that there was one (that is, a chair and a handle); putting the chain on (assuming, again, etc); dropping the latch on those locks that were not dead; and/or inserting the key in any dead lock that existed in the door and leaving it inserted, thereby preventing a copy of the key, or the original in the case where Isobel Absalon's key was not the original, from being inserted into the keyhole from the outside. Such were the options, potentially, at Isobel Absalon's disposal, assuming that the door could not be barred in any other way, either literally or metaphorically.

Leaving aside the means available for securing the door from the outside for the simple reason, to reiterate, that, rather than being interested in securing it he was interested in opening it, and opening it in such a way that it remained open, keys or no keys, to Harold Absalon on his, he felt, imminent arrival, it is perhaps clearer now why he took it to be imperative that he arrive at his side of the front door in question before Isobel Absalon arrived at her side of same and, indeed, that he arrived sufficiently in advance of Isobel Absalon for him to have time to both retrieve the keys from his left-hand trouser pocket and to unlock that door using those keys, and even for him to have had time to set foot, as it is known, over the threshold demarcated by that front door or by its doorframe and welcome mat. Were he not to secure this foothold, which is to say that were he not to have literally placed at least one of his feet over the threshold and onto the welcome mat or, in the case where no such mat existed, simply on the far side of the doorframe in question (and he knew that, mat or no mat, he would not be welcome in this establishment) in the place on the far side of that doorframe where such mats were, in a typical domestic setting, placed, then it would leave open a possibility for Isobel Absalon still to lock the door from the inside in the multifarious ways described, since there would be nothing standing in the way of the door, such as his leg, to prevent Isobel Absalon from closing it and locking it in the ways described. Such were some of the reasons for his urgency and strong desire to arrive at his (etc) side of the front door before Isobel Absalon arrived at her (as before) side of the same door, which is to say at the opposite side of the door.

18

WHAT, THOUGH, IF Isobel Absalon actually wanted him to unlock the door, he wondered, as he continued to move towards it? What if she had been incarcerated therein, with no means of escape, and had been waiting a long time for a rescuer, such as himself, to appear?

In most places it was simply a case of upping and leaving when one had had enough. One could up and leave, for instance, at any point during a dinner party, or during a party, which is to say, in the latter case, a party where a formal sit down dinner was not being served, which is not to say that there would be no food at all – the hosts may have made some slices of pizza, for instance, in the sense of having made them from the raw ingredients (flour, water, buffalo mozzarella etc), or having simply taken the pizzas fully prepared but uncooked from their packaging, and placed them in a suitably hot oven for a suitable duration, as specified in the recipe book, say, in the former case, or on the packet in the latter.

There was, of course, another position which had, until that point, been overlooked but which now emerged into his mind: the scenario of the pizza delivery. Quite simply, the pizza delivery was a case where raw materials are used, as with the 'home-made' category, although the pizza house cannot be said to be a 'home'; the origin of the vast majority of pizza deliveries was not a home but a restaurant or, in the case of the pizza house, a restaurant that does not have any seats and tables for customers' use, or, to put it succinctly, a pizza restaurant that was 'take out' or 'delivery' only. Thus the delivered pizza and the home made variety had that similarity – of being made from raw materials. That was not to say, of course, that the shop-bought variety was not made from the raw ingredients. It was to do, he thought, with who was responsible for preparation and who for cooking of the pizza in question. The home-made and the delivered variety shared the following attributes: that the person or people who had *prepared* the pizza *also cooked it* whereas in the case of the shop-bought pizza the person or people who had prepared the pizza did not cook it, except in the case of the person or people in the factory or other production facility who took one home with them, from the production line, so to speak, as it was known, for their lunch, supper or, in much more unusual cases, breakfast. In this latter (and to his mind, somewhat exceptional) case it could (and no doubt would, by some) be asserted that there his sharp delineation between preparation and cooking in the case of the 'shop-bought' pizza was undermined. That was true enough. One means of strengthening his position somewhat, he thought, as he reached further into his left-hand trouser pocket with his left hand, was to rely on the term 'cook' or 'cooks' (a reliance that implies, in the 'home-made' and 'delivered' varieties, both the task of preparation and of cooking the pizza in question); this was, perhaps, the solution to the conundrum. Was it enough, now, to assert that in the case of the home-made pizza and the delivered pizza, the 'cook' (or 'cooks') is (or are) responsible for the *preparation* of the pizza along with the other job that the title (singular or plural) implies, whereas in the case of the shop-bought pizza the cook is not responsible for the preparation? He thought it was enough, at least for now.

Then his mind went back to that troubling exception – the woman (as he imagined her to be) in the mid-lands (of whichever country she resided in), with her hair covered (regardless, he hoped, of which country she resided in), working in pizza-preparation all day and then taking one or more of her products home for lunch, supper or, exceptionally, breakfast. Ah yes, but during the process of *preparing* the pizza she could not be termed a cook, even if, at a later time or date she took one of the products of her labour home to cook it (and perhaps her company allowed their employees to do this with faulty products, or gave them a discount on non-faulty products, one of the perks of working at that facility – quite possibly the only perk). Therein lay the difference he thought: we could *not* call her a cook during the process of production, whereas in the case of the preparer of the home-made pizza, or the pizza to be delivered, the preparer, in the act of preparation itself, *could* be termed a cook. What a relief he felt at that moment!

And it was with gratitude that he turned his attention to something which so far has only been alluded to in passing: that is the scenario in which pizza (of whatever variety) is eaten for breakfast. He had, rather rashly he now thought, asserted that it was highly exceptional or just exceptional for pizza to be eaten for breakfast. Now an image came to mind which undermined this: that of the cold half-eaten pizza sitting on a plate or delivery box, which, in turn, was placed on the floor, or on a table or chair, in the bedsit or student house on the morning after, and he wouldn't specify after what but leave that to other (unspecified) imaginations.

Leaving aside the prevalence of this scenario given his previous rash pronouncements in this area, what could be said about the categorisation of this example? Firstly, the evidence at hand (that is, to mind) did not allow him to decide between whether the cold pizza would be shop-bought, delivered or home-made. However, he felt that it was unlikely to fall into the last category. Why did he think that? He would have to bring in another concept to explain himself: that concept was 'house-pride'. The term was introduced in an unusual formulation here for reasons of syntax. One cannot edit one's thoughts for the convenience of transmission, he thought. The presence of the cold pizza still on the plate or in the delivery box implied, to his mind, that the inhabitants of that house were not house-proud (to use the more conventional expression); the further implication in his mind of this lack of house-pride was that the inhabitants of that house would not be proud enough (in the sense defined) to use raw ingredients under their own hands and initiative to make the pizza that was now sitting cold on the plate or in the box (and note that the presence of the box implies, in itself, that the now cold pizza was not homemade or even shop-bought but delivered, unless, of course, the coldness of the pizza was due to it never having been cooked rather than it having been cooked and having been left to cool on that plate or in that box. In the case where it had never been cooked but was still in the box (opened or unopened) on the chair or table or on the floor of the non-proud (etc) inhabitants' house then it followed naturally to his mind that the pizza was of the shop-bought variety, which again rules out the possibility of home-making of the pizza in question). He focused, narrowing down the possibilities with his fine mind, notice, on the case of the cold pizza *on the plate* rather than in a box, a pizza that *had* been cooked. What could he say (to himself, silently, as he sped across the area in front of the townhouse) about this specimen. He would start with what he couldn't say:

he couldn't say it was shop-bought as opposed to home-made or delivered; or home-made as opposed to shop-bought or delivered; or delivered as opposed to the other two options; in other words he couldn't say whether it had been prepared by a cook (in the sense defined above) as opposed to a mid-land 'producer'. Nor could he say, at least with as much certainty, that the inhabitants of that house were not house-proud – they had used a plate or plates for the purpose of dining. Granted they had left the remains of their pizza on the plate and, in turn, on a chair, table or on the floor. But this did not imply a lack of house-pride in the way that a pizza (whether previously cooked or not) would imply if it were left in the same (or similar) position but in a box. It could simply have been that the diners had been called away by a pressing engagement or activity of some sort (such as sex) or by an emergency (such as a road traffic accident directly outside their front door, or by an upstairs fire) and that they had left the pizza in its place for that reason.

Which musings neatly brought him back to – indeed demonstrated the validity of – his first thought: that at a dinner party, or at any other sort of party where food was served or not, then one could simply up and leave if one wanted to, a possibility that would not, at that moment, be available to Isobel Absalon, in the case of her incarceration within that townhouse.

19

A KEY WITHOUT a key ring could not be fished out of a trouser pocket, he thought, as he finally made contact with the key in his left-hand trouser pocket – a key that he now urgently needed to fish out of that pocket to enable his ingress into and/or Isobel Absalon's egress from the townhouse in question. The reason a key without a key ring could not be fished out of a trouser pocket was, he thought, that, in fishing a key or keys out of one's pocket, one of one's fingers needed to hook the key ring, in a similar way to that in which an actual fish was hooked, using an actual hook, to fish it out of the drink, as it's known. One could, of course, simply grip one of the keys, or part thereof, or more than one key, or parts of more than one (etc) if there were more than one, between one's index finger and thumb, say, as a means of pulling the keys out of one's pocket, but this would *not* qualify as fishing them out, to his mind, since the resemblance between the index or other finger and the fishing hook would be absent. The action, in that case, would more resemble the mechanical grab, he thought, than the angler's hook, and it was for this reason that he had concluded, at the moment that he'd finally made contact with the key in his left-hand trouser pocket, that a single key, sans key ring, could not be fished out of one's pocket in the manner described.

A single key could, of course, be with or without a key ring in as much as it did not need a key ring to keep it together, as it were, whereas a bunch, so-called, of keys *did* need a key ring or other device to keep it together, and he was not aware of any device more useful than the traditional key ring for keeping a bunch of keys together in this way. This did not rule out the possibility that a single key would necessarily in fact be without a key ring of course; it was just to say that a key ring would not be required for a single key for the reason that a bunch of keys would need, as it were, a key ring, or other, inferior device, to keep them together. And the reason, note, that a bunch of keys needed, often, to be kept together was that they belonged to a particular person and were used by that person and occasionally, granted, by others, to unlock doors and other things such as safety deposit boxes or chastity belts [12] and not just any doors (etc) but the doors (etc) that specifically related to that person (etc). They were, then, the doors, boxes and belts through and into which that person regularly needed to gain access whilst preventing most others from doing so and, in the case of the chastity belt and perhaps in other cases, preventing *all* others from gaining access. That was why they were collected together, those keys, generally in the recommended way, which is to say using a key ring.

In his own situation approaching the front door he found that the key in his left-hand trouser pocket was indeed attached to a key ring; furthermore, this key ring contained other keys; more specifically, it contained keys that he thought would allow him to gain access to the house that he continued steadily to approach in his on-going investigation into the disappearance of his colleague, Marguerite, who was last seen in pursuit of Harold Absalon, the Mayor's transport advisor. The forefinger

12 I think it was something to do with us having been an item – and Harold having been absent – for so long by that stage. I never got a sense that she felt she was cheating on him.

of his left hand now found that key ring and 'hooked' it, which is to say that it inserted itself, or rather he inserted it, into the key ring i.e. into the area bounded by the circumference of the key ring. He then proceeded to bend that forefinger in the easiest way that he could given its anatomical constraints, which is to say that he bent it towards the thumb of the same hand, and it was this action, he knew, that had spawned, as it were, at least in part, the term fishing a set of keys out of one's pocket or fishing something out of anywhere except, perhaps, the fishing of a fish out of a pool or other body of water since that would be tautological. Of course, in the case of the fish the hole would not have existed before the insertion of the hook into the fish's mouth, unlike the 'hole', if we can call it that, formed by the key ring, which is to say the two-dimensional area bounded by the inside of the key ring, an area that is circular, or near circular, in most cases. Clearly fishing a set of keys out of one's pocket, as he now began to do, in that his finger touched the thumb and he began to withdraw the hand again from the pocket dragging the keys as it went, was a much more humane act than fishing; at least it was a much more humane act than fishing using hooks, as is traditional, to pierce the top palate of a fish as a means of hauling that fish out of the drink during the act of fishing. Regardless of this, he was convinced that the bent finger accounted in large part for the origins of the term 'fishing out', due to its perceived similarity to the shape of the angler's hook (and he preferred 'angler' to the gender-specific term 'fisherman' so as to ensure that the rare instances of female anglers were not excluded from within its compass).

He tugged on the key ring as a means of completely removing it and all of the keys attached to it from his pocket as he continued to move across the area in front of the townhouse towards the front door. Only once he had fully removed the keys and the key ring from his pocket in this way would he be satisfied that he had fished out the bunch of keys rather than still being in the process of fishing them out. The image of the poor fish flapping from side to side just above the surface, water dripping from its body back into the drink, came to his mind then. It made him feel sad.

20

NOTICE THAT HE was not panicking, despite the fact that Harold Absalon[13] was, as far as he could tell, closing in on him, as it's known, and he had still not traversed the area in front of the townhouse in question. It was with increased urgency, though, that he tugged on the key ring through which his left forefinger was now hooked, an urgency that finally yielded an object that was attached to that key ring, an object, moreover, that had been impeding the passage and ultimate release of the keys from his pocket.

He did not look down at the object as he continued towards the townhouse, and the fact of his not looking down meant that the object – a description thereof – did not enter his mind at that moment and so is not, as yet, available to us. This was not, of course, to say that, in liberating the object attached to the key ring, he had not gleaned further clues as to the nature of that object. Not all evidence is collected through the visual sense, in short. He had, then, gleaned some evidence about the item attached to the key ring in question but this evidence was, for now, purely in the non-visual domain. It could reasonably be asserted that the evidence that he had gleaned about the relative dimensions – relative, say, to most keys – of the object that had now emerged from his pocket was gleaned through

13 In fact, even she had taken to calling me Harold. The first time she had done so I felt euphoric; each time afterwards felt like a blessed relief. Our relationship – what I had started to think of as a marriage – had normalized, then, to that extent.

the sense of touch. It could not, for instance, have been gleaned very easily by the sense of smell, since this sense did not lend itself to ascertaining the dimensions of things: the sniffer dog locates the narcotics regardless of the dimensions of the haul, as the text book might express it. And similarly the oral sense – that is to say the sense of taste – could not be employed in this instance given the anatomical limitations: the object had been within his pocket whereas his mouth, which is to say the seat of his taste faculty, remained, as always, within the lower part of his head, and the distance between them could not be negotiated in the time available without doing severe damage to his person. Granted, if he had had more time available to him – and his time was constrained, remember, by the presence of Harold Absalon who was, he thought, rapidly bearing down upon him, [14] as it were – then he could simply have removed his trousers in the usual way and could have put the pocket into his mouth; rather he could have put that part of the trouser pocket containing the item under investigation into his mouth as a means of sensing the dimensions of that object. This would still not, though, be using the taste faculty to assess dimension; he would no doubt taste *something* in putting that part of that trouser pocket into his mouth, and he anticipated that the taste would be both savoury and pleasant, given what he knew about that particular area of his trousers, with its food remains and nasal deposits. No, it would still be the faculty of touch that would offer up the dimensional clues, albeit a sense of touch from inside his body and accompanied by a panoply, perhaps, of tastes and possibly even smells, given the proximity of nose to trouser at that moment. Nor could the

14 I could never shake off the prospect of Absalon's return, however, even if she could.

aural sense lend anything of itself to assessing the dimensions of the object in this instance. The sense of hearing, to express it somewhat differently, could be used to assess distance, as in the case of echo location or sonar, faculties or skills that he did, in fact, have in his armoury, should situations emerge requiring their use: his entry, for instance, into a warehouse in pursuit of a suspect intent on eluding him and, as a means of doing so, trying to remain outside of his field of vision whilst being unable to remain completely silent when moving around that warehouse or whilst trying to remain stationary within it. He was a master of detection in that situation, as in so many others, in that he could finely tune his hearing so as to use it as an instrument for locating the suspect and judging his distance from her, in the case where the suspect was female or in the case where the suspect was at least strongly suspected of being female alongside other suspicions of a criminal nature, there being no offence attached, of course, with simply being female[15] or even of simply being suspected of being female.

This having exhausted the possibilities in relation to the sense faculties at his or indeed anyone's disposal as a means of judging the dimensions of an object or more specifically of the object that had hitherto been inside the left-hand pocket of his trousers but which had just emerged from that pocket, satisfied with the further evidence that had been forthcoming from this exercise and clear, in his mind, about how this evidence fitted into his investigation into the disappearance of his colleague, Marguerite, who was last seen in pursuit of Harold Absalon, the Mayor's transport advisor, he simply glanced down at the

15 She had told me that she would never tolerate unfaithfulness. This, she said, was what had caused her mother's death: the behaviour of her father. She'd cut off all ties with him. I was left in no doubt that the same would happen to me, in the same circumstance.

object in question, as he continued to pull the key ring with his left hand or, more specifically, as before, using his left index finger as a hook through the key ring as a means of extracting the keys themselves, keys which remained, still, partially within the left-hand pocket of his trousers despite the emergence of the key ring and the object attached thereto. He glanced down, then, simply as a means of confirming what he already knew: that the object attached to the key ring was an electronic key, an electronic key, moreover, as well as the vehicle that it would open, that he suspected belonged to Richard Knox, the colleague of Harold Absalon.

21

WHAT SORT OF vehicle did the electronic key as it were belong to, he wondered, as the keys – both conventional and electronic – emerged fully from the left-hand pocket of his trousers. What, moreover, was the nature of the central locking system within that vehicle, given the vehicle-specific characteristics of such systems? In the case of the black cabs that, as it were, ferried passengers around the city that he was then inhabiting, for instance, the rear doors were locked when the vehicle was moving and unlocked when it was stationary. This was for safety reasons – for the passenger(s) themselves rather than for the safety of the public at large; the latter would be the case, it could be argued, for the centrally locked rear doors of a police car, although in the case where the police car's non-police occupant(s) was or were, in fact, innocent (in an actual rather than purely legal 'until proven guilty' sense) then it would be for the safety of those occupants in the same way as with the taxi case. In fact, even if the non-police occupants of the police car were actually guilty, the rear central locking would still serve the function of helping to ensure their own safety but with the *added* function of protecting the public at large by helping to ensure that the guilty party or parties did not escape from the vehicle, which would give them the opportunity of continuing the crime spree that they had perhaps been engaged in perpetrating until the moment of their apprehension. But in what sense could both cases be categorised as instances of central locking, he now wondered, as he inspected the electronic key dangling from the key ring? What, more importantly, were the similarities, if any, between these forms of central locking and that employed in other modes, such as over- or underground trains and trams/coaches/buses?

It was the driver, in all cases, who controlled the central locking, although in the case of the high-speed, long-distance train it was the conductor, who controlled when the doors opened; and of course there was no conductor in cars, which is to say that it was not a role ordinarily found in private road vehicles. This was not to say that conductors didn't travel by car. They had just as much right to do so as the rest of us. It was just to say that when they *were* travelling by car they were generally off-duty; and if they were *on*-duty then they were doing that part of their job that didn't require them to be actually conducting *per se* – perhaps doing an errand, obtaining some more blank tickets on paper or card to feed through their ticket machines, say, or going off to buy some lunch. There were any number of things they could be doing for heaven's sake – let's not go into that now.

The driver or conductor, then, would control the centrally locked doors of a bus, tram, coach, underground or long distance train; the driver would control the centrally locked (and unlocked) doors of the saloon, estate or other modern car – at least that subset of modern cars that actually had central locking. The two cases were, then, broadly similar to that extent, he felt almost compelled to say.

However – to move on to the key difference, to his mind – with the centrally locked train, tube, tram, bus and coach, the main issue was to control people getting *off* rather than getting *on* – just as in the case of the centrally locked police car – whereas with the centrally locked private car, lorry and van the main issue was to control people getting *on* rather than getting *off* – in other words to prevent people from absconding with the vehicle. Reasonably pleased with this, despite its evident flaws, he moved onto a much deeper question, one which he feared he would have insufficient time to fully explore: in what sense was this type of locking central? Where, in other words, *was* the centre precisely? This profound question had emerged, he thought, due to the idea of just having *centrally* locked *rear* doors, if, in fact, this was the situation in taxis and police cars. Would the centre in that case be located between the two rear doors or in the centre of the vehicle as a whole? Or did 'the centre' simply refer, rather vaguely, to the vehicle as a whole, or even to the key that transmitted the message to the vehicle, saying either 'lock up!' or 'unlock!' It couldn't possibly be the latter he thought, because what about the situation when you pushed down one of the 'knobs', in a private road vehicle and all the other knobs went down at the same time – wasn't that central locking but *sans* key? (He didn't know the French word for key.) And what about the equivalent situation in the bus, tram, coach or underground or long distance train? Did one simply take the geometric centre of the three-dimensional space bounded by the exterior of the train or vehicle, or was it preferable to use the centre of gravity, as it is known?

Frustrated by his failure to make progress in this area, he noticed that the branding on the electronic key matched that of the car that he'd seen parked haphazardly, facing, as it were, in the wrong direction, at the side of the road behind him.

22

HOW, THOUGH, DID he know that the car was facing in the wrong direction, he wondered, as he noticed that the key ring also had a metallic fob attached to it with a short section of chain? After all, cars did travel in that direction along the street that the car was parked alongside (albeit on the opposite side of the road). It must be a combination, then, of direction of travel plus side of street that was critical in these cases, he surmised, noticing that the metallic fob had a sequence of numbers stamped upon it; he must have used his expertise in this area instinctively in his determination in this instance, he thought.

But how did one know which side of the road was which, he now wondered, as he realised that some of the numbers matched those scribbled in ballpoint inside the book of matches? If you need assistance in this area then imagine, he thought, that you are standing in the middle of a conventional two-lane road and that it is a quiet road – this will help you keep your mind on the example since there's nothing quite as distracting lorries, combine harvesters and tractors passing you when you are standing in the middle of a conventional road about to be given a briefing on which side of the road is which. Note that there is no need to actually physically move any-where, unless you believe that would be of assistance to you in visualising the scenario more clearly and distinctly; and if you do feel the urge to actually move to a nearby (or more distant) similar highway (and more imaginative souls could skip the foregoing passage, he thought) then you should take care, in a number of ways: firstly you should ensure that the road is as quiet as the rural road under consideration in the imagined counterpart to your actual physical experiment; this means not too many vehicles (including cycles) – the number of pedestrians is immaterial. In fact, it would be useful to have as many as possible there, pedestrian-wise, because you would be able to pass on this briefing directly to them, that is, without bothering our investigator with it, or without them having to refer to the scenario that is currently (still geminating) in his mind – that, then, would be the most efficient means of conveying this briefing, taking as many friends and family and acquaintances with you to this quiet road so that you can demonstrate to them directly, without them having to bother themselves with the source material, as it were, how to work out which side of the road is which; you, your family, friends, acquaintances and anyone else who doesn't fall into those four categories should all wear bright clothing (this only applies to those people who are actually going on the excursion to the quiet road; other people who fall into the now five categories (which in fact now encompass the whole of humanity) but who are not going on this excursion do not need to wear bright clothing unless, that is, they have other reasons for wearing bright clothing, including safety issues related to excursions to some other road or roads, just simply the desire to be seen or the fact that wearing bright colours immediately puts them in a generally and genuinely positive state of mind); in addition, if the excursion takes place at night, then you and everyone else (defined as previously) should also affix a reflective strip to your front and rear; that is to say that you should affix one of said strips to the front of your bright clothing (your white T-shirt, say, if it is a warm evening or other period of the day that you are planning to sojourn in, or your orange coat, say, if it is a cooler period or epoch that we are concerned with here) and you should affix the other of said strips to the rear of your bright clothing (same examples as given above – in fact, it should, ideally, be affixed to the same item of bright clothing that the previous strip had been fixed to, and this should be the item of bright clothing that you are actually wearing on the excursion to the road that you have selected as being similar to our investigator's imagined example (and wouldn't it have been so much easier if you'd just stuck to that imagined example rather than going through all this rigmarole just so that you can have an actual physical experience of what is going on in his fine mind?), that is, rather than affixing a strip to the front of your group as a whole and one to the rear of your group as a whole, although this would of course serve a similar safety purpose, but only if those people who were at the front and rear of the group when the affixing was taking place remained, for the duration of the excursion, as the front- and back-markers; nor, for extra clarity, does affixing to the rear mean affixing anything to the backside – some in your group may argue that this was what was intended, and they may perhaps argue this as a means of being able to man- or woman-handle other members of the group for their own ends but you should vigorously deny it, saying that that was not what he had meant at all and that if they wanted to do that then they would have to sort out their own excursion, with all of the preparation and reference to source material that that entailed. These preliminaries having been carried out you should be ready, assuming, that is, that you have all, individually, catered for the non-safety issues of the excursion, or those areas at least that are not so directly safety-related, for, it could be argued, that making sure that you are wearing the right footwear *is* a safety issue in a sense – you could cut your feet if you fail to put on your shoes of course; similarly wearing trousers or a skirt is important, in a sense, for safety reasons – making sure that you are warm enough so that you don't catch pneumonia (or even just a cold). There are still other aspects of being ready that might, indirectly, be safety-related. For instance there is the issue of personal grooming: many people wouldn't say they were ready for the excursion unless they had combed their hair; a sub-set of this uncombed-so-unready group would even insist that they were not ready because they hadn't combed their hair even if it was an excursion in the middle of the night. Similarly with teeth brushing, although not, perhaps, with the caveat about time of day. Are these personal grooming issues also a part of our personal safety? In a sense they are, for in not taking good care of our hair and teeth we risk lice in the first instance (although it is said, not by the lice themselves but by observations of their behaviour presumably, that they prefer people with clean hair) and tooth decay in the second. He couldn't imagine that the first affliction could be fatal, although if it went on for long enough he thought it could drive you out of your mind, and he could imagine people in purgatory engaged in incessant scratching of the scalp, but he couldn't imagine what sin would have occasioned it, insufficient personal grooming not being a sin in any religion he was aware of. The second affliction, that of tooth decay, *could* be fatal, he thought – lack of a means of chewing would surely result eventually in the life force being drained away (although there was always soup, of course) – although not within the period of time it took to embark on, and return from, the excursion to the 'test road', as he now thought of it, although it was out of his hands which road you chose – it could be some distance away, in another country even, in which case combing the hair, brushing the teeth (yours and your dependents') [16] and attending to other areas of personal hygiene and grooming would be important – imperative even. All he is thinking is that he will not provide any advice on what constitutes readiness in these areas in the same way that he has given advice on readiness in the areas of bright clothing and reflective strips. The reason that he is not giving such advice is that, although these areas (e.g. personal hygiene and grooming) may pertain to safety, the way in which that safety is potentially jeopardised is much less immediate than in the case of being run over by a combine harvester, say, or other farm or non-farm vehicle, because the driver of that vehicle – the one involved in running you over – had not been able to see you until it was too late, in which case the draining away of the lifeblood might be more or less immediate and Marguerite's unnamed investigative colleague would feel responsible, even though you had acted simply on a stream of thoughts in his mind that he had not even verbalised but which had, in some way, entered your own mind as an idea generated by him. He would feel responsible in that scenario; rather he constantly, or as near to constant as is possible for him, feels responsible in thinking what he does (based on this vague incipient notion that somehow, from somewhere, his cognition *is* being monitored) that people should not get the wrong end of the stick as it is known; people die all the time, but let it not be said that he brought anyone's death forwards significantly

16 I knew that, in the absence of Absalon, I was all that she had: estranged from her father, her mother dead.

by not just taking an extra moment to define, as precisely as he possibly could, the terms that he was using to express himself during his thought processes.

Satisfied, at last, that you and your entourage would be prepared for your excursion in the right way (and with all legal disclaimers duly in place: that despite his best efforts he cannot be held responsible for any loss, damage, personal injury... etc etc) then you should set off on that excursion, if you haven't done so already. On arriving at the road you should make sure that no-one steps into it: remain on the pavement, if there is one; otherwise remain on the sidewalk, if there is one; otherwise find a place of safety, away from the road, where you and your entourage can stand – or sit, if their level of preparedness included bringing with them portable seats; or lie, if they have brought some sort of mat upon which they could do so; and even if they haven't brought anything to lie or sit on (standing not really requiring any particular piece of equipment to enable it to take place comfortably, notice, at least in many cases) they can sit or lie or stand, whatever they want to do, so long as they are not obstructing the area in which they are standing/sitting/lying, obstructing it, that is, to other people or other creatures (such as farm animals) who wish to either traverse that area, or remain within it for a time, or a combination of the two, even at regular intervals. You may have to find another quiet area of roadside in which to do this – be flexible in your approach whilst ensuring that all of the conditions set out above are adhered to (and even if they are, he cannot take ultimate responsibility for what are, after all, your own independent actions). This period of waiting is included so that you can take in the following passage, just into your mind, that is, without acting upon it, with him not being aware, remember, of how this transfer of thoughts, if that is what it is, can possibly be taking place. Leaving the remaining members of your entourage in the place of safety, look both ways along the road (the ways will be defined shortly – your purpose in being there of course). Having satisfied yourself that there are no vehicles coming then walk out into the middle of the road. If there is a vehicle coming then wait for it to pass and then follow the instructions from the start of the previous sentence. Stand astride the white line in the middle of the road facing in the direction of the white line (either one way or the other, down or up the road – those are the only options). If it is a series of lines like this: - - - - - - - - as may be the case, then choose any line that takes your fancy and stand astride that line. It is best, however, to choose a line that enables your entourage still to see you, in all your bright reflective splendour – in other words, don't go making a big deal of choosing a line and tearing half way across the countryside (along the test road that is) in doing so. In standing astride, you do not need to strain yourself (and if, contrary to previous instructions you have chosen a road with a central reservation then you should abort immediately, recap on the salient points from earlier and then find another, more suitable road). Remain alert to any vehicles that may be approaching – if you hear or see one then get out of its way as soon and as safely as possible: your enduring presence on this earth is much more important than any silly test demonstration. Then point, with your left hand to the *left*-hand side of the road and say, as loudly as possible 'from my point of view' (an important caveat that, to prevent confusion in any of your viewers) 'that is the left side of the road'; similarly (having dropped your left hand down to your side, or put it back in your pocket – having brought it, in short, back to rest in roughly the position from which it was called into action) raise your right hand, point at the side of the road to the right of your central axis, and say, more loudly now, 'from my point of view, this is the right-hand side of the road'. That will be an end of the matter for you, but you may wish to reflect on the original point: that in some states, cars (and all other vehicles) drive on the left-hand side of the road; that is, they travel, in a forwards direction, the way that you are facing, but travelling on the left of the line or series of lines that you are currently standing astride; in other states, cars (etc) travel, in the direction you are facing, but travelling on the *right*-hand side of the line or series of lines that you are currently standing (don't sit!) astride. That is all there is to it. You may wish to encourage the rest of your entourage up, one by one, taking all due precautions, to experience this simple insight from their own point of view, that is, standing astride the centre or dashed line of their choosing (they can't, of course, *choose* a centre line – there will only be one in that instance), seeing as though they have followed you out there, willingly or otherwise, to take part in this useful demonstration.

There are exceptions of course: combine harvesters and other very wide vehicles do not travel only on one side the road, they *straddle* the centre line, much as you have just been doing, at least on the narrower and quieter country roads. But the principle is the same: where they can be accommodated on just one side of the road then they will stay on the side of the road that is the ordained side for travelling in the particular state that they find themselves in. What about roads that do not have any central markings, he wondered to himself (as though waking from a long, but not particularly illuminating dream)? That is a more tricky situation. It requires one to *imagine* a centre line (which could prove tricky, to his mind, for those difficult, unimaginative people who insisted on actually getting out there, finding an appropriate road, and doing their own demonstration of the issue) and to drive to the left or right of that, according to the custom. The important thing here, if you are driving on such a road, is to ensure that if a vehicle approaches your vehicle but in the opposite direction, that either you ensure, by judgement, that you collectively have room to pass one another on the correct side of each other. And this is a key point - from her point of view she will be driving on the left, if that is the case in that particular state, just as you are driving on the left; similarly with the right; similarly also, in fact, with driving in the centre, although there are no states that he is aware of where the default is driving in the centre - it would not be a state in which the economy would flourish, he ventured, although there are some specific cases - one-way streets for instance - where the intention was that you should drive in the middle of the road, but in that case you would be unlikely to meet a vehicle coming in the opposite direction, at least a vehicle whose driver was acting lawfully, unless, of course *you* were driving the wrong way down a one-way street, as it is known, in which case you would be acting unlawfully in this, and perhaps other regards - you may have just robbed a bank, for example, in which case you would be acting unlawfully in that regard too, and this might, in fact, have occasioned your driving the wrong way down a one-way street in the first place, as a 'getaway', as it is known. Alternatively, if there is no room to pass the oncoming vehicle in the no-line two-way road scenario then you should stop, reverse, and let the other vehicle pass you at a suitable passing point - many narrow roads have passing points just for this purpose, although they may be used for other purposes too, such as parking, which, for those people who want and need to use them as passing places can be highly irritating. The other alternative is that the other driver, having stopped, reverses to his or her nearest (behind him or her) passing place to allow you to pass them. There is room for kindness here, and it brought a warm feeling to his stomach to think of you and the other motorist vying with each other to give way to the other, crunching the gear stick into reverse in your haste to serve, to defer to the other. Common sense should come into it too, however: if you know that there is not a passing space behind you for some way, or if you have a series of cars or other vehicles behind you then you should perhaps look to the other motorist to reverse; if they are in a similar predicament then they should give way to you if you are a woman and they are a man, and vice versa (and this is not to say anything about men's and women's relative capacity for reversing – it is just an echo of a previous chivalric age that our investigator continues to uphold in his mind); if you are both men then work it out amicably between you; if you are both women, simply let the more proficient driver reverse; rather, let the more proficient reversist reverse (that is, just because she's good at reversing does not mean she is the better driver overall); the driver of the car (or other vehicle) behind her will, we hope, see her 'reversing lights' and will select the reverse gear themselves – she will, in short, set up a (probably short) chain reaction which will precipitate a collective reversing to a wide part of the road, the wider portion also being long enough to accommodate all of the vehicles in the reversing column, as we now come to think of it. Then the pleasure of the ritual of thanks: as you pass the line of motorists parked, temporarily we hope, in the passing place, simply raise your hand – either hand (but not both) – to each motorist in turn, as a sign of thanks. In fact you don't need to raise your hand each time, just keep it raised until you have passed the whole line, then lower it again. Your passengers, front and rear, can do the same if they wish, although it isn't mandatory. Continue on your way until you meet another vehicle, at which time you may have to go through the whole rigmarole again.

The point is the same throughout: pass on the left if they drive on the left in that state; on the right if they drive on the right. That is really all there is to it.

And for those more imaginative souls who have skipped that whole passage – that is, the practical steps – the way to work out which side of the road is which is this: imagine yourself standing in the middle of a road facing along the road in one direction or the other. The area of the road to the left of you is the left-hand side of the road from your point of view whilst the area to the right is the right-hand side of the road, again, from your point of view. It really is as simple as that.

And for those who didn't need any assistance in this area at all, welcome back.

23

H E FLICKED THE keys – both conventional and electronic – around into the palm of his hand as he approached the central, and therefore the most exposed, part of the area in front of the townhouse. The keys felt warm in his hand and the reason for this was that they had been in his pocket and, more specifically in his left-hand trouser pocket in close proximity to his genital area, an area, moreover, that was often warm or even overly warm, in his experience. Given the conducting nature of most keys, they picked up the natural warmth generated in that area, and that was why, in short, the keys which he had now fished out of his pocket were warm to the touch, warm to his touch that is, no-one else being quite close enough yet to attest to this warmth generated by his genital area and transmitted to the keys that he clutched, remember, in his left hand.

How had he moved from fishing out the keys to clutching them in the palm of his hand? How, furthermore, would he move from clutching them in his hand to selecting the correct key, that is, the key to the front door of the townhouse in front of him? How, more importantly, would he open that front door in advance of Isobel Absalon, were she in a position to do so, both literally and metaphorically, from the opposite side of the door in question, and before his apprehension by her husband who was, as far as we know, approaching him from the rear? [17]

17 It was, perhaps, the suddenness with which it happened that had taken me aback.

He would move from fishing out to clutching using a man-oeuvre in which the whole hand simply turned, as though it were opening a door. In thinking 'as though it were opening a door' he realised that the door in question could be locked, in fact, or unlocked; the action, in short, was one akin to turning a key or a door handle – it didn't matter which. It was one in which the index finger that had been used to fish out the keys retained, momentarily, its 'hookishness' whilst the remaining fingers and thumb opened up, which is to say became less hookish without necessarily being devoid completely of any resemblance to a row of hooks. And the purpose of this opening out of the other fingers was to bring about a clear landing path to the palm of the hand for the keys; were the non-index fingers to retain their hook-like qualities too assiduously they would potentially block the clear passage of the key from the thin (or thick) air to the palm of the hand in question, which, in his case was, remember, the left. The keys, then, on emerging from the pocket had been hanging down on the hook of his left index finger, with the other fingers of his left hand wishing, as it were, to imitate their neighbour, that is, to imitate the left index finger by maintaining a hook-like appearance, and having to resist this wish in order to allow the keys – both conventional and electronic – a clear path through air of whatever thickness to the palm of the same hand, as the palm of that hand rotated from a near-vertical to a near-horizontal, upward-facing, as it were, plane. And it was this revolution of the palm from a near-vertical to a near-horizontal, upward-facing, as it were, plane that he had likened, a short while before, to the hand turning as though it were *un*locking a door with a key (note) or opening a door using the door handle expressly designed for that purpose. In both cases – that of key-unlocking or handle-opening of the door – the plane of the key, in the former example and of the handle in the latter mimicked the plane of the palm of the hand executing the respective action in that the key in the former situation moved, with the palm, typically from a near-vertical plane or axis to a near-horizontal one; with the handle – or at least with those handles possessing a clearly identifiable axis or plane, thereby ruling out circular/spherical handles, which were rife in some establishments according to his investigations – the move, typically, was the inverse of the previous example in that the handle would rest, as it were, in the horizontal plane or axis and the palm would, at the outset, adopt this horizontal plane or axis although, note, downwards-facing, as it were, and push the handle to or, at least, towards, the vertical axis (etc), in his experience, as a means of opening the door, as it is known or, at least, as a precursor to so doing and, in doing so, would itself, the palm that is, move from a horizontal or near-horizontal axis – downward-facing, as it were, as before, to a vertical or near-vertical one. In rehearsing these two examples in his mind, he realised that it was the former that provided the closest parallels to the current situation in that, in the case of the left hand being used to unlock a door using a key that was turned in the lock in an anti-clockwise direction then the palm, according to his extensive investigations, would typically move from being vertical, or near-vertical, to being in a horizontal or near-horizontal axis etc and this was very close to what had happened in moving from fishing out the keys to those same keys resting warmly in the palm of his left hand.

Would he need to take his left index finger from the key ring – would he need to unhook it, in other words – before moving onto the next phase of his operation, namely, selecting the appropriate key to open the front door to the townhouse in front of him? Yes, he thought he would need to unhook the index finger. He would need to move to gripping the key between thumb and forefinger, and he would not be able to complete this action quickly, he thought, unless he first unhooked his left index finger from the key ring. Having done so, would he actually need to transfer the keys from his left to his right hand, given that he was what's known as right-handed? It could not be ruled out. Given that time was of the essence, he now unhooked his left index finger, leaving the keys resting momentarily in the palm of his left hand and, in so doing, skilfully and efficiently opened up the next phase of his operation, with all of the dangers that that entailed.

24

WHAT IF THE locks had been changed, he thought, as he retrieved his right hand from his right-hand trouser pocket, having deposited the book of matches therein, as a precursor to receiving the keys in that hand? This procedure of lock-changing generally took place under a number of discrete scenarios, the primary examples being in the aftermath of a burglary or when a wife, generally, had uncovered her husband's infidelity. [18] Only in very rare circumstances, he estimated, would both of these situations pertain at once, although the possibility of the husband using the burglary as an attempt to cover up his own misdemeanours in some way could not be completely ruled out.

As his right hand started moving towards his left to enable the keys to be transferred from the latter to the former, he reflected further on the difference between changing the locks on the house and changing the lock to the gate, feeling certain that this would assist him in his inquiries. The difference did not just lie in the use of the plural in the former, classic case (that is, 'changing the locks') compared to the latter, which used the singular (that is, 'changing the padlock'), although there was something in this difference; the difference had more to do with the ease with which one could change a padlock securing, say, a gate, compared with the ease with which one could change

18 I returned home one evening some time later – and not long after she'd told me the good news – to find the house deserted.

the locks securing a house, other dwelling or establishment, to refer to this whole class provisionally in that way just for the moment. And that term 'establishment' did point more fully towards the difference between the two situations: the word suggested, by extension, as it were, more established practices, procedures and infrastructure for locking and unlocking those premises. This was certainly the case with the locks that had confronted him – the padlock and, a little way ahead of him, across the remainder of the area in front of the townhouse that is, the locks to the house itself, an establishment, remember, that he knew was the key, in a metaphorical sense this time, to unlocking the whole Marguerite mystery, if indeed that was what it was i.e. a mystery. In short, then, padlocks were used to secure less well-established premises, or open areas such as the area that he was currently traversing, via gates, doors or other hinged or slotted barriers (and he hoped that this last phrase would act as a catch-all, as it were, for cases where the entrance/exit-way to a bounded open area did not consist of a door or gate, although he was not clear to what specific cases this referred).

Leaving aside bounded open areas for the moment, he brought to mind instances of the former case, that is, less well-established premises traditionally secured by padlocks, and came up with the following preliminary list: sheds, warehouses, lock-ups and outhouses. Granted the first example could be encompassed by the last – that is, one could class the shed as a type of outhouse if one wished – he wouldn't stand in the way of that. And note, also, that the archetypal outhouse – the outdoor privy – probably didn't lend itself, as it were, to being secured by padlock for the simple reason, he thought, that there was nothing really to steal from such an outbuilding.

Still, he felt sure that if one were to require a secure outdoor privy then the means that one would use to secure it would be the padlock. This was in the case, note, of said privy being unoccupied of course; in the case of it being occupied then it would be secured from the inside in the usual way, with, in more advanced models, perhaps an exterior indication of its occupied status; in less advanced models the view through a gap in the perhaps dilapidated wooden door, or the sound of a newspaper rustling or the smell of cigarette or pipe smoke partially masking other less savoury odours would perhaps have to suffice as that indicator. Where there was a requirement for these less well-established premises – and he was not pretending to have presented an exhaustive list of them – to be secured from the outside they would typically – or not unusually – be secured using a padlock, with a chain, bracket or other means of attachment such that the means of entry or exit was barred, so to speak, when the door was closed and the padlock secured in the appropriate position.

Leaving aside his inappropriate use of the word 'appropriate', he returned to the main thrust of his argument, which was, remember, the relative ease with which a padlock could be changed compared to what is known as changing the locks: in the former case one simply had to go to pretty much any hardware store and buy a new padlock, which could be used as a replacement for an existing padlock provided one had the key for the existing padlock and that the key was still able to unlock that padlock, which is to say that the padlock hadn't become rusted up, say, to the extent that it couldn't be unlocked even with the correct key, or hadn't been damaged or tampered with in some way such that it could no longer be used for the purpose for which it had been designed, namely securing an outbuilding (etc). These are just examples of course – there was a myriad of other reasons why the correct, as it were, key may no longer be able to unlock its, so to speak, padlock. Of course that might be the very reason why the padlock needed to be replaced, in order to secure again, for example, an outhouse that had lapsed in use due, say, to modern innovations or – a more urgent case this – to release someone locked inside; in these latter cases the padlock would have to be broken, but, this difficulty aside, it was still easier to change even these seized-up padlocks than it was to change the locks to an establishment such as the house that he hoped soon to enter.

The relative ease related, in short, to being able to do it oneself; that is, one could generally replace a padlock oneself, especially if one had the appropriate tool along with the brawn and brains to release an existing seized-up padlock, if required. In the case of changing the locks, one generally had to bring a man in – and it was generally a man, regardless of the gender of the person desiring to change the locks. The man in question – the one who was brought in in such cases (and there is obviously more than one of these men) – is called a locksmith. In the case where the door itself has been damaged – by the burglar or cuckolded husband [19] to give the contrary side of the earlier example – it may be necessary to have the door repaired before calling in the locksmith; depending on the extent of the damage – and of his abilities – the locksmith may be able to render the repair himself as well as changing the lock(s). In the case where the wife was cheating on the husband by seeing a locksmith, a discounted or free fitting might be provided.

19 That Knox took an extended leave of absence around this time was not, I knew, a coincidence. What I was faced with was finding a way to track him down so as to find her again.

25

HE WANTED THE front door key to be primed for
use, then, at the moment when he was faced, as it
were, by the front door of the house in question. Perhaps
an *open* doorway would await him, contrary to his earlier
pontifications and predictions, when he arrived at the threshold in question. He could not rely on his. This was why
he continued moving his left hand towards his right as a
precursor to transferring the keys from the former to the
latter, as he traversed the area in front of the townhouse.
This transfer would have the obvious disadvantage of tying
up his favoured right hand as it were. Note (especially to the
rookie detectives) that this tying up should not be taken in
a literal sense. This was not to say that literal tying up had
no place in the private or even a public investigator's armoury,
as it were. It was one of a number of investigative techniques
of which he was a master.[20] No, the sense in which his right
hand would be tied up, rather than being literally bound
up with twine, rope or other binding (a noun which somewhat begged the question, he thought), related to that right

20 Strange to say my career continued to progress during this time, despite
   – perhaps even because of – Knox's absence. Some spoke of me as a
   potential successor, even though he was much better connected than
   I could ever dream to be. They asked me to take on his job, though,
   temporarily, as I continued to fulfil Harold Absalon's functions. In
   fact – bizarrely – it was Knox himself, apparently, who, in absentia, had
   nominated me to fill his shoes whilst he was away doing whatever it was
   that he was doing.

hand being otherwise engaged, would be one way of thinking about it, engaged, that is, in holding the keys – both conventional and electronic – to the front door of the house in question and to other premises, whether established or otherwise, to bounded areas and to vehicle(s) unspecified, and manipulating those keys, as he would need to do, so that he was gripping the appropriate key between thumb and forefinger of his right hand as he approached the front door and, more specifically, as the key in question approached the appropriate lock in that very door. He took, then, the phrases 'otherwise engaged' and 'tied up' to be synonymous in the situation described, namely the situation in which he referred to his own right hand, which, remember, he favoured over his left, as being effectively tied up at the moment of its carriage and manipulation of the keys in question. Being otherwise engaged got closer to what he was trying to express to himself and, somehow, to others, which was that, in judging that it was appropriate for him to move the keys in question from his left to his right hand for the short journey, by foot, as it is known, from his current location to the front door in question, this meant that his right hand would not be available for other operations, whether covert or overt. For those of a lewder mindset he wanted to distance himself from what 'covert right-handed operations' might be taken to mean. He reflected on how little control he had over how his thoughts were interpreted or, indeed, over how those mysterious trainees were acting at that very moment – for all he knew, for example, they could be engaged in covert right- (or, granted, in rarer cases, left-) handed activities in the sense alluded (or allewded) to whilst at the same time apprehending his thoughts, following in his footsteps, as it were, and this was a well-established[21] practice, he knew, in relation to certain publications. He could not be held responsible for that or for anything else that these characters were engaged in – he wanted this to be taken as a general disclaimer. His own right hand would not be available for such activities or for any activities once it had received the keys, both conventional and electronic, from his left hand given that it would be manipulating those keys such that, to address those of a lewder mindset more directly this time, the front door key, as representing the male organ, could be slid into the appropriate lock, taken as representing the female organ, such that he could gain a wider access, as it were, into the house that held the key in a different sense to the disappearance of his colleague, Marguerite, who was missing, and of Harold Absalon, the Mayor's transport advisor, who had been missing. That, in short, was what he had been trying to say (to think rather). And if the point still remains obscure to the less experienced investigators amongst you then you will have to follow it up in your own time, since he needed, at that moment, to re-engage with the situation unfolding before him given that the door within that front façade had swung open to reveal Isobel Absalon dressed in a blue silk bath robe that he knew belonged to Richard Knox. Instead of looking at the investigator standing almost on the doorstep (although note that there was no step, in this instance, to or at the door in question) her eyes widened and her lips unstuck as she looked past him towards the gate to the area in front of the townhouse. Without turning around, he knew that this must be because her husband was now at

21 This was the first time that I'd had my own office – in the corner of the block looking out over the little public square with the traffic, and the grids of government offices, beyond. I tried hard to hide how much this affected me.

that gate; he knew, too, that they were entering the final phase of the investigation into the disappearance of Marguerite, last seen on the trail of same.

26

I T WAS NOT glue that had momentarily stuck Isobel Absalon's lips together, he thought, as he let his still-empty right hand fall precipitously away from his left. If that had been the case she may not have been able to part them in the straightforward way that she had; she might, indeed, have needed to be admitted to casualty in that instance. The reason they had stuck together but were so easily parted was that she was wearing crimson lipstick, although the colour, note, was incidental to the adhesiveness (if not to his interest in them and her).

As the name suggests, lipstick[22] is a substance that sticks to one's lips thereby giving them colour; not that one's lips are entirely devoid of colour before one applies one's lipstick to them: many people's lips are, in any case, a pinkish colour, for instance, although this is far from universal; conversely, when one was on the verge of death, say, or of keeling over, then one's lips were said to turn blue, although he preferred to refer to this pre-death or pre-keel hue as blue-grey since he felt that reflected the reality much more closely. The blue-grey colour could also be descriptive of hypothermia or extreme cold, as

---

22 I also acquired Knox's secretary, Hazel, whose desk was located, guardian-like, outside the door of what I had taken to calling my office. She was conscientious, encouraging, although I got an inkling, from time to time, of her continued loyalties to him. Still, she was an asset. She knew so much about how to run things that I sometimes wondered, in running the project, who was really administering and supporting whom.

had been the case with Harold Absalon at a certain stage since his disappearance. These, then, were just two of the many naturally occurring, as it were, lip colourings. And note here the distinction that he had made between the natural and the artificial – he consciously avoided the pejorative term 'unnatural' – which he was using to differentiate between those lip colours that one's own body produces, so to speak – that is, consciously or unconsciously – and applies – without application, that is – internally but which are, of course, visible externally otherwise, of course, they could not count as 'colourings', and those lip colours which are artificially produced by others but generally applied to oneself by oneself. However, this did not exhaust the meaning of the term 'natural' in relation to lip colourings, since included within it are all substances found in nature lending themselves to lip colouration, such as the secretions of certain flowers, and it was in this sense that the crimson colouring on Isobel Absalon's lips could be taken to be natural – in other words it had been produced from mostly naturally occurring products but not internally (i.e. not by her).

This self-applied crimson lip colouring had a stickiness that enabled it to adhere, for a time, to one's lips, and it was this stickiness that had held the upper and lower of Isobel Absalon's lips together momentarily as she opened her mouth on seeing her husband, presumably, in the area in front of the townhouse. In a sense, it was not an intentional feature of lip colourings, he thought (nor was the adherence of some of the colouring to the teeth, on occasion, giving the impression of carnivorousness once the mouth had performed the task of opening sufficiently to reveal the teeth in question). Instead, this capacity to stick the lips momentarily together was a by-product of the need for adherence to each lip separately in order for the product to function according to its remit. A final note in the area of lipsticks came into his mind: the term 'stick', here, referred, he thought, to this quality of stickiness but also to the supposed resemblance of the lipstick item itself to naturally occurring sticks e.g. the stubby debris of a tree found on a muddy path after a blustery night. However, this latter link was tenuous, he thought, to say the least, and he left it to one side, as, managing to avert his gaze, finally, from Isobel Absalon's luscious lips, [23] he commenced his ascent of the stairs leading up to her.

23 There was no suggestion of any sort of impropriety with Hazel, by the way. I was on the brink of something momentous, career-wise, after all. People perhaps already suspected me of an involvement in the disappearances of both Richard Knox and Harold Absalon, not to mention an entanglement with the latter's wife, en route to this corner office-with-a-view, a space within which I was seemingly making myself at home.

27

H E S W E P T U P the stairs to the front door of the townhouse, his left hand returning, now, palm upwards, with
the keys – both conventional and electronic – towards his left-
hand trouser pocket.

Having said that he swept up the stairs, now, to the open
front door of the townhouse, there would seem to be an inevitability, for those of us now familiar with his investigative technique, that there would be, on his behalf, an inquiry into what
it was he had done in that instant – what, in fact, he was still
doing, given that he was still in the process of sweeping up the
stairs in question towards the front door in question. And that
inevitability stemmed, he thought, from our familiarity with his
method of attempting, to the extent that he could, to clarify his
terms, often as he went along, to ensure that he left no stone
unturned, was perhaps how the training manuals put it, in his
investigations, and, in the current instance, in his investigation
into the disappearance of his colleague, Marguerite who, presumably, had been so formative in instilling this investigative
technique into him in the first place. He could not then, given
his training and mentoring, and his experience, thus far, in the
field, as it were, sweep up the stairs in front of the townhouse,
towards Isobel Absalon, with Harold Absalon now, he sensed,
having entered the area in front of the townhouse behind him
(meaning that, presumably, he was now actually amongst us)
without really nailing, as it were, what, in fact, he was doing

in sweeping up those stairs in front of the townhouse in the way described.

He was not, of course, literally sweeping up those stairs, in the sense that he did not have a broom, or a dustpan and brush, was not using some or all of those implements, if that was what they were, to systematically sweep or brush the horizontal and perhaps even the vertical planes of those steps as he went, as a means of removing, or at least moving, dust and debris from those surfaces as a means of cleaning them, or even of *spring* cleaning them.

No, he did not have those, or similar, implements in his possession as he swept, and continued to sweep, up those steps leading from the area in front of the townhouse in question to the front door of same, which, was standing, rather than, say, lying or sitting, open; but it was not for that reason alone that he was not sweeping up those stairs in the sense of using those or similar implements to remove dust and/or debris from the horizontal and perhaps even the vertical planes of those steps, assuming such dust and/or debris to be present, which it wasn't. Even, then, were he to have had a broom and/or a dustpan and brush in his possession as he swept up those steps (and he refused to countenance the dustpan not being together with the brush, which was why he had not used the 'and/or' between the 'dustpan' and the 'brush'; they should, he thought, remain together at all times – they depended on each other in that beautiful symbiotic relationship that we are all, hopefully, familiar with to some extent) then it would not have been in the sense of actually using those implements in his on-going movement that would have formed the main part of his rationale for asserting that he had swept or, rather, was sweeping up those steps, and the reason that it would not have been in the sense of actually using those implements on one or both of the planes of those steps (with, he thought, their use on the horizontal plane being a minimum requirement) was, quite simply, that he was in the middle of an investigation that was becoming more fraught by the moment, an investigation, remember, into the disappearance of his colleague, Marguerite, last seen on the trail of Harold Absalon, the Mayor's transport advisor, who had been missing, and one that, somehow, he knew he was entering into the final stages of. Given the fact, then, of his on-going investigation, and the fact that he was entering into the fraught yet crucial endgame of same, then it would seem wholly inappropriate to him, his superiors – even his inferiors and peers (and we can put ourselves in whichever of these categories we think to be most appropriate) for him to engage in some cleaning and tidying, regardless of whether: the action was or is unfolding during the spring, summer, winter, or fall; there is or was debris present on those steps; and he has or had a dustpan and brush, which, remember, should always *always* be kept close to each other, and/or a broom in his possession at that moment.

This was not, of course, to say that one investigating a disappearance or other crime should never use these implements during a live, as it were, investigation (and he wasn't referring to the similar, but generally smaller implements that were often used at the scene by his forensic colleagues, such as the fingerprint brush, an analogous but opposite situation, this latter, in that the fine particulate matter would be introduced into the picture as it were, before being swept away, rather than simply being swept away); it may be, in a particular case, that adopting the identity of, say, a road sweeper would be the best undercover means of observing covert criminal activities that one would not be able to observe were one to be wearing the traditional investigative garb of trench coat and Fedora; one should not rule out, in other words, swapping a trench coat, Fedora and newspaper for a donkey jacket (the leatherette shoulders being, to his mind, optional) and broom, if the situation demanded it; it was just that the current situation did not demand it – in fact, it would be positively counterproductive given the nature of the current investigation and the stage it had reached for him to suddenly start sweeping in that sense, with or without the roadsweeper's traditional apparel.

It was not, then, in any of these senses that he had swept, and continued to sweep, from the area in front of that townhouse, up the steps leading towards the front door of same, a front door that still stood (etc) open. It was, rather, in the sense that he was travelling at speed, along, and up, the aforementioned trajectory, and it was, perhaps, this speed that had as it were precipitated this comparison with sweeping in that, in both activities there would be, if one looked closely enough, swirling, dusty eddies on either side, with, he thought, the clockwise eddy being on the right of the person sweeping, in whatever sense, now, you want to take it, and the counter-clockwise eddy being on the left of that person (assuming, as always, that, given we are following in their dust-free, now, footsteps, that we are facing in the same direction as they are). It was, then, simply a sign of the speed with which he was now moving, with this speed a consequence, of course, of the precarious position he now found himself in and the enormous potential for his investigation into the disappearance of his colleague,[24] Marguerite, last seen on the trail of you know who,

24 No, I didn't want to fuel further speculation by anything untoward with Hazel. I did, though, want to find an early opportunity to probe her, subtly, on Richard Knox's whereabouts. There was still some unfinished business there, after all.

that was afforded to him by travelling at such speed whilst retaining the clarity and meticulousness to which we have now, he hoped, become accustomed.

28

THE FRONT DOOR stood open to him then. The sense in which it stood rather than, for example, sat partially open to him related, he thought, to its resemblance to the human body when in standing posture and, more specifically, to the *average* human body when in standing posture. He had copious evidence at his disposal to suggest that, just like a door, an average human subject – when standing – was taller than it was wide and was wider than it was deep, which is to say that its vertical dimension was larger than its horizontal dimension and that its horizontal dimension was larger than its depth. And this was regardless, he thought, of where one measured those as it were human dimensions from and to: one could, for example, measure depth along the soles of the feet; from rear end to front of penis, regardless of whether the latter was erect or in a flaccid or semi-flaccid state; from small of back, as he thought it was called, to protuberant belly button, and in the situation of a withdrawn belly button, to the belly surrounding that button, as it were; from the back, mid-shoulder blades, to the fully erect female nipple on the more sizeable of the two breasts where there was a noticeable if not significant difference in size between them. Wherever, in short, one measured the depth of the average human subject, it would still be less sizeable than the horizontal dimension of the same subject was his submission, as, closing his left hand around the keys – both conventional and electronic – in their journey back to his left-hand trouser pocket, he stepped past Isobel Absalon and into the house; similarly with the horizontal dimension in relation to the vertical, using whichever bare extremities take your fancy; and it was the resemblance of these dimensional relationships between the door and the average human subject when standing that had enabled him to assert that the door in question, which he continued to pass on his left, with Isobel Absalon on his right, was standing, rather than, say, sitting open.

In asserting that the door stood open he was not denying that the way now *lay* open before him. In this latter case he took it to be the resemblance between the way ahead in the sense of the trajectory of his, and he hoped Isobel Absalon's, onward journey as it were, and the prone human form, whether average or not, that provided the correspondence of terms, which is to say, our ability to use the word 'lay' in relation to both the way ahead and the prone human form, whether below-, above- or just plain average. And the reason that the stipulation about averageness, to coin a term, was not required in the case of the way lying open to him and others related to the fact that even the fattest person, whether lying on their front, back or side, whichever was most comfortable for them, could be taken to lie in a way akin to the sense in which the way lay ahead, for what he hoped were reasons that were now obvious, at least to his more imaginative and/or technically astute followers. But would this still hold, he now wondered, if the way that lay ahead of him took in the stairs just inside the door to the left. He pondered this whilst simultaneously, or near simultaneously, wondering if Isobel Absalon was holding any implement in one or both of her hands that when delivered with force to his head, as may have happened previously, would send him sprawling, prone, unconscious, probably in a forward direction such that he might lie lengthwise along the way that lay open to him and would thereby be prevented temporarily or permanently from going upstairs with Isobel Absalon, which, he now realised, was his greatest wish and which he knew might provide him with the final clue to solving the disappearance of his colleague Marguerite, and the relationship between the disappearance and that of Isobel Absalon's husband, Harold Absalon, the Mayor's transport advisor, who had been missing.[25] He did not turn to look at Isobel Absalon; instead he continued to focus on the way ahead, whilst returning in his mind to whether, when that way ahead included a flight of stairs, as they are known, as it did, he knew, in the current case, the resemblance between that way and the fattest human form in a prone position still stacked up, as it were. His question could perhaps be re-expressed in the following way: when leaning forward resting their massive belly against that flight of stairs did the fattest human subject more resemble someone lying or standing? In other words, wouldn't the fattest human subject whilst resting their enormous gut against a particularly steep flight of stairs more resemble someone standing rather than someone lying down? And if this were the case then could one still refer to the way, taking in those steep stairs, as lying

25 The decisive lead came to me one morning when, for whatever reason, I followed a different routine. Ordinarily I would leave the empty Absalon house early, there being nothing there to keep me. On this occasion I was somewhat later and I approached my office via a different route: instead of passing through reception, saying good morning to Sophie, the receptionist, who had taken to calling me 'Sir', I entered through the door in the opposite wall of the lift lobby – this so as to be able to walk through the whole open plan section of the office (a) to see who was in at that time of morning (not many) and (b) to greet those who were in early, this to help with morale and to show my face to the people, to encourage them – what's known as the human touch.

rather than standing in front of one? Continuing to move into the house, turning to look, just with his eyes, at the actual stairs in question, and continuing to remain conscious in the absence of any swift arm movements from Isobel Absalon or any other factor that might render him unconscious, whether temporarily, as had occurred, he now thought, at the outset of his investigation, or permanently, he concluded that if the stairs were not particularly steep, as in the current case, then even the fattest human subject could be taken to be lying on them rather than standing against them and that he could continue to refer to the way as lying ahead of him – as well as the door standing open to him – even if that way lying ahead took in those stairs as he hoped they would for him and for Isobel Absalon, if not for Harold Absalon, with all the promise that that way ahead would provide in this continuing investigation into the disappearance of Marguerite who, for all he knew, was still on the trail of Harold Absalon, the Mayor's transport advisor.

29

H E HAD LEARNT, even in his earliest training, that it
was necessary to take in a scene in all its detail, especially when one was coming to the end of one's investigation,
so that one could brilliantly relate, whilst referring to each of
the clues, how one had constantly stayed one step ahead (as
before) of even the archest of arch-criminals, with all of the
dark ingenuity at their disposal. When all of the suspects were
gathered together, which only ever occurred at the end of a
case, one could demonstrate to everyone present how observant one had been and, moreover, how one had seen the real
pattern linking all of the key items in question, rather than the
pattern laid down as a decoy by the criminal fraternity – the
sub-set thereof involved in that particular case – or any other
pattern, whether the work of a criminal or other mind or no
mind, which is to say a pattern of man, of nature, of chance, of
fate or of God, if one believed in any or all of those latter sorts
of things. But it might be asked how, precisely, in his case, he
knew that he was coming to the end of his investigation and,
for that reason, knew that he needed to amass the final clues
leading to a conviction, such as the detailed arrangement of
items on the telephone table to his left and the fact that there
was what's known as a decorative fish eye mirror on the wall
above this table. Wasn't it actually easier for *us* to know that
his investigation was coming to a close, given the thickness or
thinness of the remaining evidence, as it were, he wondered,

somehow, to himself as he noticed, in the decorative fish eye mirror, his own resemblance to Harold Absalon, the Mayor's transport advisor? [26] And if, as he strongly suspected, he did have superior or preferential knowledge relating to the final unfolding of the investigation, given his unsurpassed experience and training in this area, and that this superior or preferential knowledge resulted in a deeply felt instinct that the investigation would finally unfold in the bedroom on the first floor of the house in question in Isobel Absalon's presence, whether clad or unclad, then how did that instinct, so deeply felt, square with our own *knowledge* of the thickness or thinness of the remaining evidence, so to speak, he wondered (assuming that the majority of those following his investigation are doing so in a traditional way that our investigator can only be distantly aware of if he is – or was, rather – aware of it at all, rather than following his progress on a screen, say, and he didn't mean, in this case, a CCTV screen)? We are supposing a lot, he submitted, as he continued to move towards the foot of the stairs, in somehow holding that our own evidence on the likelihood of an imminent conclusion to his investigation was more reliable than his own; and the main thing that we are supposing, he asserted, was that the evidence that we have at our fingertips is all of the available

26 What this meant was that I approached my office from the opposite corridor leading to that corner. It was for this reason that Hazel did not apprehend my approach, even though, ordinarily, she was so vigilant, on my behalf. I caught her unawares, momentarily. She was with an administrative colleague – someone from accounts whose name I should have known – and they were looking at one of the glossies that report tittle-tattle about the nonentities that, in this country, pass for what we call celebrities. As I passed them, and they closed the magazine in embarrassed silence, I was sure I saw a picture of Isobel with Richard Knox getting out of a very plush-looking motor car in ball gown and dinner jacket, looking very pleased with themselves indeed.

evidence. Who of us is to say that what we have is all there is, in other words (even if we do have access to the previous volume)? Granted that were there to be subsequent evidence submitted to us through whatever form, that his reputation for completeness and for providing satisfaction as an investigator would be very much on the line, as it were. Now it might be fine to submit, somehow, an erratum or errata to his evidence should that prove necessary – that, he thought, would prove acceptable although it would be undesirable to a perfectionist such as himself. This wouldn't matter much, he suspected, were he to complete his investigation in a timely fashion such that he would provide satisfaction to those shadowy figures such as yourself somehow following in his footsteps; and what this meant, he thought, was, quite simply, solving the mystery of the disappearance of Marguerite, his investigative colleague, using all of the evidence at his and our disposal and doing so in the most elegant and unlikely way possible such that none of us could ever have guessed the outcome even though we have had access to precisely the same evidence as him. Moreover it involved completing his work in this way without the need for any se- or prequels or any other subsequent sub-mission more sizeable than the single sheet of an erratum, should this, for whatever regrettable reason, prove necessary. He knew that a few blank pages at the end of his submission would be satisfactory to most of those following him in the traditional way, especially given that this could be used to record their own evidence as the investigation has unfolded and will continue to unfold. Such was the pressure on him as, starting to rotate his left hand clockwise, as it approached his left-hand trouser pocket, he continued towards the stairs, noticing that telephone was surrounded by an address book open at the letter Q, a Yellow Pages open, implausibly, on the page relating to private investigators, and an unopened packet of Senior Citizen cigarettes.

30

I SOBEL ABSALON'S WHOLE body turned as he continued to walk past her. The way in which it turned was
clockwise, which is to say that, when viewed from above, Isobel
Absalon's body turned in the same direction, although somewhat more swiftly, as his left hand and, more classically, as the
hands, as they are known, of an analogue clock. Meanwhile his
own body had started to turn in the opposite direction, which
is to say that his body had started to turn anti-clockwise or in a
counter-clockwise direction, depending on your particular con-
tinental sensibilities and preferences of expression, as he started
reaching towards the banister with his right hand. His body
had started to turn in an anti- or counter-clockwise direction
because the stairs to which he was headed, as it is known, lay
to his left and he needed to align his body such that it would
be moving towards those stairs – the first step, at least – on that
stairway, and the way in which he effected this reorientation
was by turning his body in an anti- (etc) clockwise direction
such that its momentum would take him towards the stairs, all
else being equal or at least all else, including Isobel Absalon,
not conspiring against such a manoeuvre and movement. His
left hand turning clockwise whilst his body – the remainder
thereof – turned anti- (etc) clockwise was dictated, then, by
the requirements of his investigation, which he intuited, with
all the investigative experience behind this intuition, were best
served by his depositing the keys (as before) in his left-hand

trouser pocket whilst ascending to the first storey of the house in question and entering the bedroom of that property, ideally with Isobel Absalon (leaving aside, for the time being, any mention of the bed [27] itself, whether king-, queen- or some intermediate size, or some size of a smaller or larger dimension than any of these foregoing examples). As well as being dictated by the requirements of his investigation, the speed with which his left hand revolved clockwise whilst the remainder of his body revolved anti-clockwise, was also affected by a new piece of evidence that presented itself to him just at that moment: the telephone on the telephone table at the bottom of the stairs started to ring.

27 My research – at the National Newspaper Library – led me to a most disturbing place. It appeared that the societal outings of Richard Knox and Isobel Absalon had commenced much earlier. It would seem (and I found this particularly sobering – chilling, really) that their relationship had started long before Harold, even.

31

T HE NEW EVIDENCE – that of the telephone starting
to ring – had affected his speed of revolution, as has
already been stated, which is to say that it had affected the
speed of clockwise revolution of his left hand as well as the
speed of *counter*-clockwise revolution of the remainder of his
body; what has not been indicated is how the speed of revolution had been affected; that it had been affected has, in short,
been established just not how, then, it had been affected... in
short, the speed of revolution was increased, rather than de-
creased, in both instances, by the onset of ringing. That was
what he had noticed. He wondered to himself, as he continued
revolving (and walking, note, still, towards the stairs) whether
the speed with which he was walking was also affected by the
onset of the ringing emanating from the telephone sitting on
the table designed, perhaps, for the purpose of hosting, as it
were, that telephone or any other similar appliance, hence the
name that he had given it in his mind, namely, 'telephone table'.
And he noticed that the speed at which he was walking, as
opposed, note, to revolving both his left hand and the remainder of his body, although he was engaged in all of these motions
simultaneously, as has already been established, had indeed
been affected by the onset of ringing. How, he wondered, had
this particular motion been affected? Rather, how had the
speed at which he was engaged in this motion of walking
towards the stairs been affected by the telephone sitting, as it

were, on what he supposed to be a purpose-built table at the bottom of the stairs, starting to ring, he wondered, in what was becoming a thoroughgoing review of his actions at the moment that the telephone in question had started to ring? In short, his speed had been adversely affected, albeit momentarily, by the onset of ringing from the telephone. And what he meant by adversely affected, those two words that he had just filed in his report reviewing the incidents precipitated by the telephone starting to ring, was that he had slowed down, momentarily, on hearing the ringing of the phone sitting, so to speak, on the table that he took to have been designed for the purpose of hosting, as it were, the phone located at the foot, as it is known, of the stairs that he hoped soon to ascend. He noticed the presence, however, in his own report on this matter of the word 'momentarily'. What he had intended in his use of this word was to indicate that although at the moment of hearing the phone starting to ring just to his left that his walking speed had been reduced, that this reduction in speed had not continued beyond the moment that he had first heard the phone ringing. In exploring his statement more fully in this way, and more specifically exploring his use of the word momentarily contained in that statement, he had clarified his submission to the extent that it was now more apparent that the speed at which he had been walking had been adversely affected (as before) for the duration of that moment; what he had not clarified in this branch of his inquiry into the disappearance of his investigative colleague Marguerite, last seen on the trail of Harold Absalon, the Mayor's transport advisor, was whether his walking speed at the end of the moment defined above had simply reverted to its pre-existing value, which is to say whether he had re-commenced walking at the speed at which he had been walking immediately prior to the onset of ringing from the telephone or whether the speed at which he had continued walking after those moments of slower walking associated with the onset of phone-ringing was higher than at the moments before the phone had started to ring (etc). A re-expression for the purposes, he hoped, of greater clarity: had he sped up after having momentarily slowed down, the latter slowing down having been brought about by the telephone ringing (etc)? Before filing a submission responding to this branch of his inquiry, he felt the need to explain, as he continued to walk at a still undisclosed speed and revolve in direction(s) and relative speed(s) that had been disclosed, why the alternative of him having slowed down further rather than resuming his pre-existing speed or increasing it had not been investigated in the foregoing. The reason that he had not investigated this outcome and had not made a submission, until now that is, within his report into the aftermath of the onset of phone-ringing, as he now chose to refer to those moments, was, he thought, perhaps obvious to the more astute trainees following his investigation through whatever mysterious (to him) means at their disposal. For the less advanced – or less experienced – trainees he spelt it out: the reason he had not investigated this outcome was indicated by the juxtaposition of the words 'adversely affected' – or, more specifically the word 'adversely' with all of its negative connotations – with the word 'momentarily'. Given that he had a negative view of his slower speed at the moment of his apprehension of the ringing phone and the implication that this slower speed had been brought about by his surprise that the phone had started to ring at that moment then isn't it obvious that an operative of his statue would at least wish to retain his composure, as it were, following that moment of being so uncharacteristically off his guard, as it could perhaps be referred to, and that one means of regaining this composure would have been to resume the walking speed that had been in play immediately prior to the phone starting to ring or his apprehension thereof? That, then, was one alternative available to him – that of acting as though he had not been startled by the phone ringing and acting as though nothing untoward had occurred by, as quickly as possible, resuming the walking speed that had been in operation up until the untoward occurrence that he was pretending was nothing untoward as far as he was concerned. The other alternative within this frame of reference was to have sped up, that is, to have increased his walking speed, following the moments of slower walking, and he knew that this would be indicative to Isobel and Harold Absalon, and any other on-looker, whether real like Isobel and Harold Absalon or imaginary, like yourself, that the telephone ringing had somehow changed things for him in relation to his investigation into the disappearance of Marguerite, his investigative colleague, last seen on the trail of Harold Absalon, the Mayor's transport advisor. And he now submitted that rather than returning to his pre-existing walking pace, to refer to it, now, in that way, he had indeed quickened his pace in response to the phone ringing, that is, after he had regained his composure, the loss of which had resulted in a momentary slowing down in his walking speed as submitted in previous evidence. He also confirmed, at that moment, to himself and to any others who, through whatever means mysterious to him, had access to this evidence, that this increase in his walking pace, corresponding, as it did, to an increase in the speed of revolution of his left hand in a clockwise direction and of the remainder of his body in an *anti-* (etc) clockwise direction *did* indicate that the ringing of the phone changed things for him in relation to his investigation. He was not keeping these circumstances from those following in his footsteps; it was just that those circumstances remained at the back of his mind, as it is known, for now, which is why we cannot yet see them, as it were. Instead of bringing them out, he continued, for the time being, monitoring the speed of Isobel Absalon's clockwise stationary revolution and his own accelerating counter- (etc) clockwise revolution combined, as it was, with the clockwise revolution of his left hand as well as his acceleration towards the foot of the stairs, noticing – or sensing, rather – and not for the first time, that the reason that Isobel Absalon's body was turning in a clockwise direction was that Isobel Absalon was monitoring his progress with interest as he walked towards the foot (etc) of the stairs within the house in question continuing his investigation into the disappearance of his, and Richard Knox's, erstwhile colleagues.

32

H E CARRIED ON walking towards the bottom on the
stairs, a place that is also called the foot of the stairs,
whilst abruptly terminating the counter-clockwise revolution
of his body. The fact that this location on the stairs referred
to two different areas of human anatomy he put to one side for
the moment and perhaps forever. There was a further item on
the telephone table, which is to say on the table designed for
the purpose of hosting, as it were, items germane to the making
or receiving of telephone calls including the telephone itself;
indeed without the telephone, all of the other paraphernalia of
phoning would be largely but perhaps not entirely redundant.
The further item on the telephone table was what is known,
at least in some circles, as an answerphone. The purpose of
this device should be self-evidently apparent, he reflected in
his continuing journey to the bottom or foot of the stairs,
even to those just setting out on their journey of training in
the dark arts of the detective. He put the answerphone in the
same category of device as the teasmade, and the reason he
did this related to the respective names of these two devices,
in that they both described, although to differing extents, the
purpose for which they had been designed: to spell it out, the
answering of a telephone in the former case and the making
of tea in the latter (leaving aside the differences in tense in the
two cases). Before expounding further upon this theme, he
noted to himself that the presence of an external answerphone

of this sort (and teasmades were always external in this sense, soon, perhaps, to be defined) meant that, provided that it was switched on, that the volume setting was high enough and that Isobel Absalon did not cut across or behind our investigator to actually answer the phone before the answerphone cut in, as it were, which was looking unlikely at that moment, then, having perhaps heard the recorded message, he would be able to hear the incoming message as it were, and this would provide a further clue that would perhaps point towards the circumstances of his colleague, Marguerite's – and, of course, of Harold Absalon's – disappearance.

Why did he think it unlikely that Isobel Absalon would get to the phone to answer it before the answerphone cut in, as it is known, he wondered, as he terminated the clockwise revolution of his left hand, which was very close, now, to his left-hand trouser pocket? The reason he thought this unlikely related to his presence within the house. It was not that he thought that Isobel Absalon was worried that it would seem rude for her to answer the phone when a guest had just arrived. Some hosts would still answer their telephones in the presence of guests, whether newly arrived or well-established, which is to say, in the latter case, well ensconced in that place of residence, workplace or other location; and those hosts who did choose to answer their phones in the presence of whatever category of guest would fall into two broad categories: those who would take the call and engage in it as though their guests were not present at all – and he attached the label 'rude' to this sub-set of hosts; and those hosts who would take the call, perhaps because they were in the habit of always answering the phone, whenever it rang, regardless of the presence or absence of a guest or guests, but would take the call simply as a means of informing the caller at the earliest opportunity that they had guests or, in the case of a call taken within the business environment, that they were in a meeting (and that was how the presence of guests would find its expression, often, in the business context, when answering a telephone call, as being 'in a meeting'). It was not, then, that he thought that Isobel Absalon was concerned to avoid being put into the category of 'rude' in the sense defined adequately enough a few moments before in his mind. He thought, rather, that the way in which his presence would preclude Isobel Absalon from answering the phone related to the surprise that Isobel Absalon must feel at his presence in the house in question, which is to say in Richard Knox's house. Was it sufficient to say, then, that it was the unexpected nature of his visit that meant that Isobel Absalon would not, in his estimation, cut in front or behind him to answer the still-ringing telephone before the answerphone cut in, as it is known? He concluded that the surprise element, to call it that, of his visit was not, in fact, sufficient to prevent the answering of the telephone in the manner described. What was missing, he concluded, was an account of the *significance* of his visit, from Isobel Absalon's point of view; he judged that the significance of his visit was such as to outweigh the significance of any phone call that Isobel Absalon might take at that moment. Was the unexpected nature of his visit unimportant, then, he wondered, as he continued his journey to the foot, base or bottom of the stairs? It was not *un*important, he concluded, but it was less important, at that moment, than the significance of his visit for Isobel Absalon. Granted that the element of surprise may actually have predominated initially in preventing Isobel Absalon from answering the telephone, which is to say that Isobel Absalon may have been stupefied on seeing a detective of his stature entering the area in front of the townhouse and this may have had the effect of bringing about hesitation in Isobel Absalon's mind in relation to how to act or even in relation to how to think. However, given that those initial moments of surprise had presumably taken place on the initial apprehension of him by Isobel Absalon from the first-floor bedroom window, a location, remember, to which he was headed with her, he hoped, in his wake, as it were, and that Isobel Absalon, in descending the stairs, not in any su-pernatural fashion but simply by walking down them, had had enough time for this initial surprise to pass and had even had sufficient time, in his estimation, for the surprise arising from the presence of Harold Absalon in pursuit of him to sufficiently subside, assuming that Isobel Absalon had not seen Harold Absalon until she had opened the front door, such that it was unlikely that Isobel Absalon's actions would still be governed in any meaningful way by this sense of surprise at the arrival of those particular guests, and that was why our investigator had given a much higher weighting to the significance of his pres-ence in Richard Knox's house when analysing whether Isobel Absalon was likely to cut in front or behind him to answer the ringing telephone before the answerphone cut in (etc). In short, he felt sure that Isobel Absalon afforded a much higher significance to the presence of such a well-respected detective in Richard Knox's house, especially one being pursued by her husband towards whom all of that detective's colleague's ener-gies had been focused for some considerable amount of time, and it was this, rather than a stupefying sense of surprise, that would, he estimated, prevent Isobel Absalon from answering the ringing telephone. Were the sense of surprise to still be fresh, as it were, then he could not so confidently assert that

Isobel Absalon would not cut in front or behind him to answer the telephone before the answerphone cut in and the reason for this was that he could not be confident about how long Isobel Absalon's hesitation, based, as it would be in that case, on a momentary, note, stupefying sense of surprise, would last. His confidence that any sense of surprise had sufficiently abated was based, then, upon the amount of time that had elapsed between Isobel Absalon's visual apprehension of the arrival of her guest(s) but also upon his knowledge of the nature of Isobel Absalon's mind, knowledge acquired, somehow, during the course of his investigations into the disappearance of his erstwhile colleague, Marguerite, who remained a missing person even though he felt sure that Isobel Absalon and the house they were currently both inhabiting would yield clues leading to his discovery.

What he had on file relating to Isobel Absalon's mind was that she was an intelligent woman. He had somehow accrued information suggesting that Isobel Absalon was quick witted, granted that the wit that could so speedily be employed was often of a somewhat mordant flavour, but nonetheless she wasn't the opposite, which is to say that he knew that Isobel Absalon was not dull-witted. Hers was a vivacity that would translate quickly into action and this knowledge of Harold Absalon's wife also fed into the conclusion that Isobel Absalon would not cut in front of or behind him to answer the phone (as before) and this final, he thought, expression of the conditions upon which this conclusion was based coincided with him passing Isobel Absalon, a physical action that made it highly unlikely for different reasons that Isobel Absalon would cut in *front* of him whilst making it more likely, were she to want to answer the telephone (etc), that she would cut or, given sufficient elapsed time, simply walk behind him to the telephone table to answer the phone in the usual way, and he hoped that these reasons were sufficiently obvious not to warrant a separate branch of inquiry on his part.

But how long would the telephone ring for, he now wondered? A lesser sleuth might conclude that, given the number of storeys in the building, as observed previously from the exterior, that the telephone would ring for some considerable amount of time before the answerphone cut in, as it is known, this to allow sufficient time for one of the residents of the house in question, such as Isobel Absalon, to descend the stairs in the mundane fashion previously described, to answer the telephone, assuming they wished to do so, before the answerphone cut in (as before), although he knew that there *were* no other residents of that particular dwelling. Furthermore, in another example of what set him apart from more run-of-the-mill investigators, as they are known, he had information to suggest that the telephone would not ring more than four times before the answerphone cut in. The information that he had at his disposal was that a second telephone existed in that property, a telephone, moreover, that was on the same line such that it would be ringing at the same time as the telephone just to his left at that moment. This drastically reduced the ringing time required since it reduced the distance of travel necessary for the resident answerer: there would be a telephone less distant than this ground-floor one when Isobel Absalon or Richard Knox were in the upper storeys of the house. In a further revelation of his investigative prowess, he knew that this telephone happened to be located in the first-floor bedroom to which he was headed with, he hoped, Isobel Absalon. All of these factors synthesised in his mind as he continued, in the moments between the second and third rings of the telephone, to move towards the foot (etc) of the stairs leading, he hoped, to the conclusion of his investigation.

33

NOTE THAT IN the case where the household in question had two phones on the same number, that one still only ever heard the phone ring, never the phones ring. Someone might ask, if they were in a part of the house where they could only just hear those phones ringing 'is that the phone?' – it would always be in the singular, in other words, rather than the plural, even if that person knew that in that household there were two phones (or more, if it was a very large household). Similarly, if, say, the father was in the bath or smoking a cigarette on the loo (he couldn't very well do both at the same time) and the child (assuming there is one in the scenario that we have just entered) should be answering the phone then it would have been absurd for the father to shout out 'Answer the telephones Nathaniel!' (assuming, for the time being, that Nathaniel is the child's name). The reasons that it would be absurd for the father to shout this were numerous but the main reason related to the difference between (how to put it?) physiology and audiology. One could quite easily *hear* the two (or more) telephones in the household if one were positioned say, mid-way between them, but just because one could be in a position to hear them both didn't mean that one was in a position to answer them both, at least not at the same time, and given the scenario under consideration here – that of two (etc) telephones being in the same household and on the same number, then there was little value in doing so at all, because all you would hear at the other end of the line (it actually must be a series of lines, when one thinks about it) was the same voice asking to speak to your father or mother or whoever they would be wanting to speak to.

Coming back to the question of physiological versus audiological constraints: there was, on reflection, no physiological constraint to answering two telephones at the same time *per se*, regardless of whether they were on the same number of not. There was a physiological constraint, he thought, to answering *more* than two telephones at the same time, but not in answering one or, at a push, two telephones at the same time. Now, if the two telephones were on different numbers (which in the scenario currently under investigation we have established they are not, i.e. they are on the *same* number) then there might be a *cognitive* constraint to answering them both at the same time. In fact, even in this situation there wouldn't even be a cognitive constraint to answering them both at the same time. Indeed (he now realised, as his left hand plunged, with the keys – both conventional and electronic – into his left-hand trouser pocket) there would be no physiological, audiological or cognitive constraint to answering two or, indeed, more telephones at the same time. He elaborated on his position in this way. Imagine a bedroom with a shiny pink eiderdown and with a line of, let's say, ten telephones lined up against the wall. All of them are a deep green colour; all have what would now be considered as the 'old fashioned' dialling mechanism. They all ring at the same time; in fact, it is a feature of phones that are on the same number that they ring synchronously (that's what he thinks, although he hasn't tested it under laboratory conditions); even if they're not on the same number then imagine they all ring at the same time, whether precisely synchronously or not. What the son or daughter does is this: as quickly as possible s/he lifts all of the receivers and places them, mouthpiece facing towards him- or herself, on an empty (up until that point at least) telephone table in front of them; then, quite simply, s/he, in their best and loudest telephone voice says 'Hello?' or '21419' or whatever else they normally say in answering the telephone. Now – and we may have got this point only on a technicality – the son or daughter would, in acting thus, have answered all of the telephones at the same time. Granted he or she would not then be able to maintain a conversation, especially not if the telephones were all on different numbers, or five were on one number and five on another, or four were on one number, three on another and three on another, or two were on one number, two on another, two on another, two on another and two on another or one was on one number, three were on another and the remaining six on another, or four were on one number, three on another, one on another, one on another and the final one on another number, or seven of the telephones were on one number and the remaining three were each on different numbers or, to leave it at that for the time being, any other combination you care to think of. Technically they would have been answered.

In reaching this conclusion he had moved through a number of manifestations of the physiological limitations of answering more than one telephone. Initially he pictured the perhaps typical scenario in a suburban or rural homestead (one that contains two phones on the same number, coming back to the original scenario under discussion): that in which one phone is, say, downstairs in the hallway and another is upstairs, say, in the bedroom. This would be a not untypical situation given the conditions of time (epoch) and geography (nothing to add) that we have established. The very fact that the purpose of having two phones was to be able to answer one of them, the one that was closest, without having to go a long distance, or such a long distance, meant that it was very unlikely that one would locate the phones next to each other, or at least not very close to each other – that would defeat the object (which is ease of answering). Given these circumstances, the initial thought in his mind was this: given the average reach of human beings, that is, their arm span; and given the fact that those human arms, whether at full stretch or otherwise, did not have the power to see or, in fact, hear, to locate a ringing phone (what he is picturing here is the son or daughter, having been called by the incommoded father, running obediently to the phone in the parents' bedroom, it being the nearest one to the room (his or her own bedroom) from whence s/he came, and then, wishing to follow the instructions faithfully (i.e. 'answer the telephones!'), with one hand poised on the bedroom phone, reaching out with the other hand to try and answer the *down-stairs* phone). It is apparent, even to the stupidest person, that it just can't be done. *Those* are the physiological constraints that he had been thinking about in the first place. Even if one had an arm (or two) that could extend and stretch downstairs to try to answer the downstairs phone (and what a circus act that would be) then by the time that that arm had groped around trying to find the phone (the arm having no sense other than that of touch) then the person on the other end of the line (or, more accurately, lines) would surely have hung up (as it's known). Someone whose neck also stretches so that they could leave one hand on the upstairs phone then *look* around the corner whilst they reached down to pick up the downstairs phone, you say? That would be utterly daft, beyond all belief.

Even so, if the call had ended by the time the father had again pulled up his pants, zipped up and exited the bathroom then there would be no way that he would know whether the child had answered the telephones in this way. He would just have no way of really knowing whether, miraculously, the child had performed the task that he had set them, probably.

Our investigator had moved from this typical (to his mind at least) scenario to whether there was anything *essential* in the situation that prevented one from answering the two (only) phones at the same time. His conclusion here, as you may have followed, was that, no, actually there was nothing in the situation *per se* that prevented one from answering two telephones at the same time. Perhaps, for some reason, the cohabiting married couple liked having the phones next to each other on the (perhaps slightly larger than normal) telephone table downstairs: perhaps they were still in the early stages of their marriage and they couldn't bear to be out of one another's sight; perhaps, in other words, they had had two phones purposefully installed side by side *so that they could answer them at precisely the same time*; perhaps they wanted to speak to their friends and family together whilst also being able to gaze lovingly into each other's eyes; you can't deny it was a possibility, although it was unlikely to be the most usual arrangement. In that scenario it was possible that the child, obeying the father (who was in the loo) and helping the mother (who was, say, in the kitchen with the radio on, preparing that evening's meal), could have rushed downstairs and, with one hand on one telephone and the other hand on the other, could have picked up the receivers, put one to each ear, and answered in the way traditional to that household or to themselves – there was nothing to prevent that, was there? The only fly in this particular ointment, which may have already been spotted, was the presence of the child themselves. It was only really plausible that this dual-phone scenario could be imagined as taking place in the very early years of marriage, before the resentments and inevitable recriminations had set in and the cohabiting married couple had started hating the sight of one another. It was one of those ideas, then, that, at the time, in the great flush of young love, would have made perfect sense but which, as time went on would have seemed more and more eccentric – crazy even. Would a cohabiting *newly* married couple in this scenario (i.e. having two phones side by side so that they could gaze away and play footsie with each other as they chewed the fat) really have a child of an age that could run downstairs and answer the telephones? Although he thought this highly unlikely given the social constraints of the time he could not completely rule it out. Perhaps the child was from a previous marriage – but even then surely the divorcee (or is it divorcée?) would know that two phones, side by side, spoke of temporary infatuation cooling to, at best, a mild indifference and, on that basis, would surely have suggested that the more traditional form of one up one down would have been much more acceptable, given their experience in that first marriage, however short-lived. It could have been a terrible scenario in which mother or father in that marriage had been killed in some way – say killed in childbirth (this would apply to the mother only) just as the full flourishing of their love was taking place. What if the husband in that situation then (well, a few years later) married the woman's identical twin who, up until that point had been left on the shelf, belying the widespread myth that identical twins always get married at the same time, in the same chapel, other place of worship, registry office or other place registered to administer such wedding ceremonies, and always to a pair (what else could it be?) of identical twins although (generally) of the opposite sex? Couldn't it then be imagined that that first flush of love, which had been temporarily interrupted by grieving and loneliness, would suddenly be reignited in the identical form of the twin sister? Wouldn't it then make perfect sense, in a way, to have identical phones downstairs, as a celebration of that still new (but redirected) love and also as a symbol of, and memorial to, twin sisters who had loved each other, despite one of them having, unconventionally, been left on the shelf when the first got married? Wouldn't that simple image of two telephones side by side then speak so much of the lack of bitterness felt by the second twin having been left on the shelf, and of her love for her new husband and child, who would, by this stage, be at least four or five years old and would therefore be able to answer the telephones in the fast-approaching reiteration of the previously mentioned scenario? It would communicate volumes on the recovery of the widower husband and of his love for his new bride, identical to the previous incarnation. And no-one could accuse him of trading the first one in for a younger model. The post mortem (or autopsy if you prefer) would be clear: natural causes. In fact, it could be that the telephones had already been installed by the husband, perhaps as a coming home gift to the mother of his child after she had delivered, so that they could transmit the happy news in tandem, a gift that she was never destined to see.

With these rumblings we satisfy ourselves, perhaps, that there is nothing inherently difficult about answering two telephones in the same household at the same time, whether or not they were on the same number or on different numbers; in other words there were no inherent physiological constraints to doing so – most of us at least had two arms to pick up two receivers and two ears to listen to them with; and, with two mouthpieces aimed at our mouth (singular), there was nothing to stop us from answering these two telephones at the same time. Really it just depended on where the two phones were located when they rang, synchronously.

There would be a cognitive constraint, he felt, if the two phones were on different numbers because the two people at the end of the line(s) would almost certainly embark on different (although perhaps only subtly, to start with) conversations which the brain couldn't process in a parallel way. It was possible, of course, that there was only one person at the end of the line(s) who had telephoned both numbers at the same time, perhaps as some sort of strange practical joke, and would then proceed to speak into their two mouthpieces at the same time; in this scenario there wouldn't be any real cognitive problem in answering both phones at the same time since the same information would be transmitted to both receivers. That would be quite unusual, though, he felt.

He had also reached the conclusion, then, that the act of answering the phone can be interpreted quite narrowly: the simple act of picking up the receiver and saying 'Hello' with a questioning tone of voice was sufficient to his mind. This was what had led, in his mind, to the situation that amply demonstrated the point – that memorable scene of the ten telephones in the bedroom. The move was from thinking that since one only had two ears (most of us) that one could answer a maximum of two phones at any one time (taking the other physiological caveats as read) to realising that the constraint, in answering the phone, was on being heard rather than on oneself hearing; in other words the numerical limitation on number of ears was no limitation at all – the only real limitation was to do with having a voice loud enough to be heard by all of the different receivers at the same time (alongside the practical issue of picking up those receivers and answering in sufficient time for the person or people on the other end of the phone not to have hung up in frustration or confusion at the delay in answering their call). That, in essence, was how his thinking had developed on this issue, nay, *flourished*.

34

H E FOUND THAT his posture, having passed Isobel
Absalon, was one of simultaneously reaching in a number
of different directions, and that this reaching could be taken
both literally and metaphorically: he found himself continuing
to reach towards the banister with his right hand whilst his
right foot started passing through the air towards the foot or
bottom (etc) of the stairs alongside which the banister ran, so
to speak; his left ear, especially, but not, of course, exclusively,
was reaching out, as it were, towards the ringing telephone
to his left so as not to miss the critical moment when the
answerphone would cut or click in whilst his left hand had
entered his left-hand trouser pocket to deposit the keys – both
conventional and electronic – in that pocket; and the gaze from
his eyes – the right, particularly, but not exclusively (as before)
– passed behind Isobel Absalon, now that their juxtaposition
allowed for this to happen, and through, note, an open door,
the presence of which had only recently become apparent to
him, an open door which led, moreover, into what looked like
a sitting room or lounge, which he noticed, despite the dimness
with which that room was shrouded, contained a number of
items which he would no doubt come on to describe in due
course.

How, though, firstly, had he failed to notice this room
until now, and, more importantly, perhaps, to his investigation, what did it mean to have noticed an open door in the

manner described? More specifically, how, he wondered, could one suddenly become aware of an absence, as in the situation from a few moments before of becoming aware of the open door through which he continued, still, to peer, whilst continuing to reach in a number of different directions as before? In his case it was not that he had expected to see a *closed* door behind Isobel Absalon. He had, he realised, expected to see a continuation of the wall which he sensed to be present to Isobel Absalon's left without having actually looked directly at that wall, focused, as he had been at that moment, on the foot (etc) of the stairs and, more latterly, on the telephone table and the contents contained thereon. It was only now that he had actually passed Isobel Absalon that he was in a position to notice the absence of what he had expected to be present i.e. the absence of the continuation of the wall and, more specifically, that this absence was not an oversight by the builder or architect (or both) but was designed-in, as it is known, to the extent that without this aperture, it would have been extremely difficult to enter the room in question (although there were, of course, the windows). Rather than an oversight, then, the presence of this absence showed considerable foresight, one could say, on the part of the architect, probably, and possibly also on the part of the builder in question in actually following the plans given to him, no doubt by the architect. That the door in question was painted a similar shade to the surrounding wall and that it opened inwards from a fulcrum on the left side of the doorway were the main considerations in accounting for the fact that someone as observant as he was – and there were few, if any, who were more observant than him, he thought (although he would, of course, include his missing investigative colleague, Marguerite, in this category) – had failed to appreciate that, rather than continuing behind Isobel Absalon, the wall in question contained this open aperture, this absence that he had so recently noticed; in other words, although it had been possible for him to have noticed the open doorway had he cast his eyes above Isobel Absalon's head and in the direction of that doorway as he had crossed the threshold into the house in question, the fact that from that angle, or thereabouts, he would have seen the top of the door itself, which was a similar shade to the wall surrounding it, even though the door was in fact open (had it been open when he'd first entered the townhouse?) and even though the doorway was demarcated by a frame in the traditional manner, the similarities of the shade involved and the fact that his mind had been focused on other more pressing matters had meant that he had not made that observation at that time but was only making it now. That he was making it only now at least had the advantage to him of being able to take in, in one go, as it is known, all of the salient features of the doorway, the door and of the items contained in the room itself: two suitcases, perched, as it were, upright on the carpet between settee and coffee table, one of the suitcases larger than the other and, lying flat on the coffee table itself, a shiny briefcase, closed, alas, which meant that he could not catch a glimpse of what it contained, whether it be used notes, a pistol plus silencer – housed, as is so often the case, as it were, in shaped slots in a bespoke foam interior – gold bullion, the key to a safety deposit box or simply the office equipment and accoutrements required by Richard Knox in fulfilling his functions and responsibilities in the project office – and, in the latter case, that equipment and those accoutrements, presumably, that needed, for whatever reason, to be carried back and forth between place of residence and place of employment in fulfilling that particular employment role.

Tempted as he was to divert his investigation in the form of his actual physical presence towards this newly discovered room and the most noteworthy items contained therein he retained the discipline for which he had become justly renowned and, whilst starting to turn his head back towards the stairway to which he was headed, noting that the third ring of the telephone had just come to an end leaving open the possibility of the cutting or clicking in of the answerphone at any moment, his right hand made contact with the cool, dark wood of the ornamentally carved finial at the top of the banister post.

35

WITH HIS HAND still on the finial, his head still turning back to face the stairs, his right foot flying through the air just above the hallway floor towards the first of those stairs, and his eyes not quite facing forwards, although he had sufficient peripheral vision to feel confident that this foot would land safely on that stair, he heard a sound which was unmistakable: he heard, in short, a baby crying somewhere in the house, which immediately brought into question whether the baby was, in fact, the offspring of Isobel Absalon and Richard Knox, rather than being Harold Absalon's.

The crying was coming, he surmised, his head continuing to swivel back, his foot continuing to fly, from behind a closed door on that very ground floor. He concluded that he would have to amend his mission parameters at his earliest opportunity – that is, perhaps, as soon as his right foot had found a firm footing on the first stair, or thereabouts – and that it was in the direction of the crying baby that he would need to head, as it's known. At the same time he knew that, rather than in the first-storey bedroom, it was within the room from which the crying was emanating that he would unearth the circumstances surrounding the disappearance of his investigative colleague, who had been on the trail of Harold Absalon, hitherto purported to be the baby's father.

What was also open to being questioned, he conceded, as he removed his now empty left hand from his left-hand trouser pocket, was the convenience with which the baby's cries, which were currently being masked by the telephone in its fourth ring-cycle, had emerged. Was he simply trying, now, to avoid further stairs, given that Marguerite, his investigative colleague, who had disappeared, had spent such a large and recent part of his own investigation already scrutinising these rudimentary elevatory devices? Was Marguerite's successor, then, using the advent of the baby's cries as a means of justifying his avoidance of what might be considered old ground, as it is known? If so, was it his judgement that he felt would be questioned, which is to say his firm, now, resolution not to ascend but to remain on the same level as the child whose cries he could barely still hear given the other elements in the sonic environment? In other words, would he leave himself open to the accusation that he had refrained from ascending the stairs, using the crying as an excuse so as not to bore, through further painstaking stair-analysis, those following in his footsteps, even though he knew that such an ascent was the best and most appropriate means of unearthing the circumstances surrounding the disappearance of the very colleague who had undertaken such insightful analysis? Or was he concerned that he would be accused of an even graver charge: of somehow conspiring with the powers that be, whoever they were and however contact with them could possibly have been made, to *put* the child in that room and to have the child start crying at that very moment to avoid those stairs? 'Did you conspire, in short, to place a child in a downstairs room in that house and for that child to start crying just at the moment when you were about to start climbing the stairs to the first storey of that house and, if so, did you conspire in that way so that your investigation might remain of interest and would not be too repetitive or boring to those who were somehow following your investigation of your colleague's disappearance whilst also having followed his investigation into the disappearance of Harold Absalon, the Mayor's transport advisor?' would be the question, he feared.

But he has no means of hearing this question, or apprehending it in any other way. At least he has no way, in his current predicament, of hearing such a question from us. The reason he has no way of hearing such a question from us is because we have no means of access to him, no means of transmitting such a question to him despite following in his footsteps all this while, and this is not just because he is located within an unnamed townhouse in an unnamed city. If he had provided an address, or even a description of the former – that is, of the townhouse in question – then we might have a chance of gaining access to him since it would provide a starting point in helping us to narrow down the options regarding which city he is located in (and notice the assumption inherent in the use of the present tense there), whereas the latter – the city state in question – would only assist in broad terms and, given that there are many more townhouses per city than there are townhouses of a given description in all of the world's cities then that latter situation would be less helpful to us. If, then, we had access to a description of the townhouse, or its address, even, then we could perhaps start to go about trying to locate the city in question; if successful, we might be able to gain access to our hero, perhaps with the assistance of legal advice on his situation provided by a 'brief', as they are known in certain circles. But the foregoing questions of city and townhouse and legal briefs (so to speak) are, remember, resting on very unstable foundations – in fact, some would say that the foundations are non-existent. It was established early on in these conjectures that the reason that he has no way of hearing such a question from us ('Did you conspire, in short, to place a child in a downstairs room in that house and for that child to start crying just at the moment when you were about to start climbing the stairs to the first storey of that house and, if so, did you conspire in that way so that your investigation might remain of interest and would not be too repetitive or boring to those who were somehow following your investigation of your colleague's disappearance whilst also having followed his investigation into the disappearance of Harold Absalon, the Mayor's transport advisor?') was because we had no means of access to him, was how it was put, and this is *not just* because he is located within an unnamed townhouse in an unnamed city – there are, in other words, other reasons why we cannot gain access to him, reasons that should be immediately apparent to most; so, even if we could pinpoint the city and townhouse in question and find and appoint an appropriate legal brief then this would be, quite simply, futile (at least it would be futile to the extent that we are undertaking these activities as a means to the end of being able to ask him our question – the activities may be useful for other, secondary reasons). It is just not worth the effort.

Fortunately we do not have to go to the lengths listed above. The reason we do not have to go to those lengths is that the foregoing was all taking place in his mind. Granted, it was a different type of reflection than those which had gone before; this does not rule out the possibility of its having occurred in his mind rather than someone else's – who else is there, indeed? It occurred in his mind as, in a sense, did this sentence. Thorny issues indeed. Suffice to say, for the time being at least, that his predicament had precipitated a new means of reflection in which he put himself to one side or (to use, instead, the vertical axis) he sees himself from above, from a god's (or bird's) eye view. This is not to rule out the other eye of the god or bird in question, it is just a figure of speech. Note, also, that that the bird's eye view rules out the bird walking past him down the corridor – the bird, in other words, must actually be in flight to be a candidate for the expression 'bird's eye view'; the gods or, simply, God, is always, he thinks, taken to reside in the heavens, so is always, he thinks, taken to be looking down on us (although, given the evidence of what he is looking down on, many justifiably doubt this or even deny it) and so the caveat is not required in that case. He (not He) was engaged, then, in a form of objective mental reflection, seeing himself as a character in a novel, momentarily; and maybe this form of reflection had been brought about by the impending end of his investigation – he wasn't sure why that would be the case but one can't deny it as a possibility. In other words, there is no 'we' in his mind, at least not one that he can rely upon or be sure about. So when, in the foregoing, the question 'Did you conspire, in short, to place a child in a downstairs room (etc),' that was, in a sense, just a form of mental play in his mind, play that perhaps arose given the pressure he is (or was) increasingly under. Perhaps he'd just started to wonder how it would feel to have a friend or friends watching him do this. It is fortunate, then, that we don't have to find a way of asking him this question – it has already been asked (several times, in fact, now) and we can simply sit back (whoever 'we' are) and wait for an answer to it.

Having somehow been asked the question, he would retort, he thought, with a further question: in what *sense* was he being accused of placing the child in the room and making them cry – an objectionable accusation for anyone to face, but especially so for someone of his standing? Was he being accused of placing an *actual* child in an *actual* room and making them *actually* cry, he wondered? If so, he would ask the judge and jury to kindly show him where this actual room and actual child actually were so that he, judge and jury could actually hear the actual crying. If in response to that retort the judge, jury or both asserted that because these actions took place in the past tense, as it were, it was not possible to go to the room and find the child still crying within it, he would respond, in turn, by asking judge and jury to at least locate the room within which he was being accused of placing said child and making them cry. He knew that they would not be able to locate the room – if they tried to locate an actual room and travel there to show him and each other then they would be travelling to as many locations as there were jurors/judges. Nor would they be able to identify the baby, even taking into account that the baby might now, with the passage of time, be an adult or even an old person – they may even have died, unsuspiciously. In short, under this dispensation both the room and the baby would be figments of their collective and individual imagination(s) – that was what he would hope to prove under cross-examination.

And if he was being accused of placing an imaginary child in an imaginary room then in what sense was it imaginary, he would ask, he thought, as the shadow of his right foot became smaller and smaller – *he* imagined – as that foot approached its landing point on the first stair? Were they, whoever they were, accusing *him* of imagining the child and the tears? Were they also, in fact, accusing him of imagining the room within which the child was crying?

Given the foregoing, in what sense could he be accused of conspiring to place the baby in the ground-floor room and at the key moment making them cry, just to avoid a repetitious and potentially boring stair ascent? Had he arranged for a man or woman, whether real or imagined, to take the child to that room and prod them at the key moment or make them cry at that moment in some other way? He had no doubt, as his foot touched down on the soft stair carpet, that the case against him would fall apart under the weight of such considerations. Freed of a sense of needing to respond to his accusers, with a final thought that maybe those accusers were themselves a figment of his own imagination, he paused, momentarily, to wait for the fourth ring-cycle to complete itself so that he could apprehend more accurately from where the crying arose before the answerphone cut (etc) in to potentially mask, in a different way, the sound of Isobel and Harold Absalon's child, or Isobel Absalon and Richard Knox's child, crying in a closed but hopefully unlocked and ventilated room on the ground floor of that very establishment.

36

THAT THE CALLER left no message but instead chose
to replace the receiver at their end with a heavy click –
even before the recorded voice had come in – was of keen interest to our investigator, in his continued reversal from a position
of having been about to ascend the stairs to the first floor of
Richard Knox's home. What was of even more interest to him
was that the phone started ringing again almost immediately
after the caller had hung up, as it is known, such that the
answerphone had not even finished its whirrings and re-wind-
ings before this new ringing had started. Why this immediate
recall, he wondered, the tips of the thumb and index finger
of his right hand still just touching the finial in their passage
away from it? He knew, of course, that he was making an
assumption in using the word 'recall' in the foregoing passage
of thought; more specifically, he knew he was making an assumption in his use of the prefix 're-' in the foregoing passage
of thought, with its implication that the previous caller – the
immediately prior, preceding one to those moments unfolding
just inside the front door of Richard Knox's house, if that was
what that property was – had immediately redialled Richard
Knox's house (etc), perhaps using the 'Redial' button on their
phone for this very purpose. The two questions that came to
his mind at that moment, as every part of his right hand lost
contact with every part of the finial so that the former was now
floating free through the air, as it were, with Harold Absalon

now, he was sure, standing behind and to one side of him in the doorway within that very property, were (a) why had he made the assumption that it was the previous caller, which is to say the immediately preceding caller, who had called back so soon after their previous call and (b) assuming that it was the previous, immediately prior caller who had called back, then why had they done so?

The caller, on encountering an answerphone message, immediately replacing the receiver, lifting it again immediately and immediately calling back, as it is known, perhaps with the assistance of a 'Redial' button on their own phone for this very purpose was a form that was very familiar to him. But its familiarity to him was not the only reason that he took it that the same caller in this instance had immediately called back in the manner described. He would not have got where he was in his profession, if one could call it that, by observing an incident and simply fitting it to previous similar incidents that he had observed, assuming that it was of their ilk, as it were. That was not to say that he was unaware of the resemblance of this particular instance of the caller, on encountering the answerphone, hanging up and immediately calling back, with the general form of such instances. He was well aware – or simply just aware – of this resemblance, as is perhaps clear. What further evidence, then, had he added to his pattern-matching, if we (he) can call it that, between the particular and general instances to conclude, or rather, to assume, that the caller in question had redialled? The further evidence in question was his very presence in that property, a fact he felt sure had precipitated the redialling in some way and it just re-confirmed for him that he was indeed on the right track in his investigation into the disappearance of his colleague, Marguerite, last seen on the trail of Harold

Absalon, the Mayor's transport advisor, and that he should redouble his efforts to move towards the room in that house occupied by a crying baby who may, in fact, be the offspring of Isobel Absalon and Richard Knox, rather than of Isobel and Harold Absalon. The caller, he felt sure, must be trying to warn Isobel Absalon of our investigator's approach and it was for this reason that they had redialled, perhaps fearing that he was already within the house and was within hearing range of the answerphone, as was, of course, the case, and refrained from leaving a message for this reason, that is not wanting to alert him that he or she – the caller, that is – had been wanting to alert Isobel Absalon of the imminent arrival of our investigator at that location. But why, if that were the express purpose of the call, had they in fact hung up and then, of course, re-dialled in the manner described? Had they suddenly found out somehow that he was already in the property and, for that reason, refrained from leaving a message? The very fact that Isobel Absalon had not answered the phone was sufficient, he thought, as the heel of his right foot elevated with the sliding passage of that foot backwards towards the edge of the bottom stair, to indicate to the caller that they were too late with their call – that he had already entered the house, meaning that the call alerting Isobel Absalon to his imminent arrival was already too late. But, if this were the case, would the caller immediately call back, he wondered, rhetorically? The reason, he held, that the caller would call back immediately was that the caller hoped that by the very insistence of the immediate call-back Isobel Absalon would intuit the urgency of the call and would, in spite of his presence within the demesne of the house, choose to ignore this presence for the duration of the time that it took her to answer the phone and, more explicitly, would use that duration to actually answer the phone. The caller had, in short, redoubled their efforts to warn Isobel Absalon about him just at the moment that he had redoubled his own efforts to move towards the room containing the crying baby and, he hoped, the solution to the conundrum of the disappearance of Marguerite, his investigative colleague. And note that this redoubling on his part was the same redoubling as previously; he had not, in other words, now increased his efforts by a factor of eight; no, his efforts remained quadrupled, this quadrupling implied by the attachment of the prefix 're-' to the word 'doubling', implying, as it did, a previous doubling, just as in the case of the redial implying a previous dialling.

How did he know that this particular instance of redialling didn't belong to another class of redialling altogether? How, more specifically, did he know that this redialling belonged to the class of 'urgent caller wishing to speak to an actual person rather than a machine' rather than to the class of 'diffident caller not enjoying speaking to a machine but would do so if they had to,' or the class of 'indecisive caller not thinking they would leave a message but then, immediately on hanging up, deciding that they would leave a message after all'? How could he be sure that the caller in this instance didn't, in fact, belong to both of these latter classes: that they were, in other words, a diffident *and* indecisive caller, even if they were not diffident and/or indecisive in non-phone-related matters, but that they had overcome their phone-related diffidence and indecisiveness sufficiently, having hung up, to decide immediately to redial and leave a message, or, if they had not overcome their phone-related diffidence and indecisiveness had at least been able to hold those qualities in abeyance, momentarily, whilst re-dialling Richard Knox's number? And in the latter case of holding these qualities in abeyance rather than overcoming them (with the implication, in the latter case, of greater decisiveness, resolve and follow-through) how could he know that they would hold their nerve as it were on this second occasion of dialling and actually now leave a message? He had to confess, at that moment, as his right heel continued its elevation and the ball of that foot continued its reversal towards the edge of the lowest stair, that he didn't actually know that the caller in question had redialled in order to communicate the urgency of the call to Isobel Absalon rather than redialling after initial diffidence or indecisiveness or both and it was for this reason that he would have to wait and see whether the caller actually left a message on this second occasion of dialling and, if they did leave a message, how this message pertained to the disappearance of his colleague, Marguerite, last seen on the trail of Harold Absalon, the Mayor's transport advisor, who had been missing.

37

THE BALL OF his right foot continued its journey towards the edge of the bottom stair until it had crossed that edge leaving just his toes in contact with that step. Even these, he found, before too long, had crossed that threshold, had moved over the edge of that step. They did so one-after-the-other, rather than all at once. And the order in which they crossed that threshold, one-after-the-other, rather than all at once, was starting with the little toe, then moving on to the next largest, then the next largest; finally the big toe and the toe next to it crossed the threshold near simultaneously, so that was where his assertion that the toes had crossed that line one-after-the-other fell down, as it were. But he did not pick himself up on this slip of the mind for the simple reason that he felt it would not be of benefit to his investigation, at least not immediately; another reason why he did not pick himself up on this slip was that, as he swivelled his body, opening up his chest, his right hand moving from the finial at the top of the stair post, Isobel Absalon walked past him through the hallway towards the sound of the baby crying. Was she doing so, he wondered, out of maternal concern? Or was this manoeuvre simply designed to thwart his own efforts to move through that same hallway and down the corridor so as to enter that room, a room that he sensed contained the solution to the strange conundrum of the disappearance of Marguerite and, perhaps, the previous disappearance of Harold Absalon, the Mayor's transport advisor? He could not wait until the next chapter to discover the answer to these and other questions; instead he acted immediately, instinctively: the way in which he acted was to change the trajectory of his right foot, mid-air, as it is known, such that, instead of that foot tracing a path towards a position adjacent to his left foot, he as it were reprogrammed the mission parameters of that right foot such that its projected landing point would be a location between Isobel and Harold Absalon on the hallway floor. Now he knew that in reprogramming the parameters relating to this part of his anatomy (and if only he could reprogramme all parts of his anatomy in this straightforward way!) that fine judgements were required if the outcome were to be as he wished: namely the right foot landing between Isobel and Harold Absalon on the hallway floor. The reason that fine judgements were required in this area was that Isobel Absalon was not stationary and he judged that even if Harold Absalon were now stationary then this situation would not pertain for long given that Isobel Absalon had just walked through that hallway towards the sound of the baby crying. He judged, in short, that his mission to unearth the circumstances surrounding the disappearance of his colleague, Marguerite, depended upon him interposing himself between Isobel and Harold Absalon in their journey towards the child. Given this moveable feast, if one can call it that, then he could not be sure that by the time his reprogrammed right foot had changed trajectory from a general backwards movement (from his viewpoint) to a more sideways movement (again, as before) before landing on the hallway floor, that the foot in question would interpose itself between Isobel and Harold Absalon. In other words, even though his right foot was now travelling at some speed through the air, albeit still, momentarily, in a generally front-to-back rather than the required left-to-right trajectory given that its reprogramming had not yet quite reached the necessary nerve endings in that peripheral location, he could not be sure that by the time it had landed in the aforementioned location, a location we could perhaps imagine as marked out on the floor of the hallway in question with the outline of a right foot with the initials 'RF' written within it, akin, to spell it out for the slower-witted amongst us, to the situation with the helicopter landing pad's outline and 'H' symbol painted within it, that Harold Absalon would still be in the location that he was currently occupying next to the front doorway. He sensed, he hoped again in short, that, even though he had let his own right foot know that it did not have time to land in the space next to his left but would need to change its trajectory mid-air so as to avoid this adjacent stopover to the left but to move directly to a position that he hoped would intervene between Isobel and Harold Absalon, that Harold Absalon may have overtaken him before his right foot landed, in which case he – our investigator – would have lost any advantage accruing from having interposed a part of his anatomy – the right foot with its associated leg, all or part thereof – between Isobel and Harold Absalon. He felt, in essence (to express, in a different way, the brevity towards which he was aiming) that unless he – and in particular his right foot (etc) – acted swiftly, that Harold Absalon would overtake him before he could ground that right foot in a position between the latter (that is, Harold Absalon) and Isobel Absalon. That was why he had acted with the speed with which he had acted on seeing Isobel Absalon pass him through the hallway; similarly that was why his right foot was travelling so quickly through the air towards its new destination which, were the respective positions of Isobel and

Harold Absalon to remain not too dissimilar to their respective positions in relation to him at that moment, would be between wife and husband, to use that shorthand.

This was not to say, he thought, as the answerphone ceased its rewinding, the phone continued to ring and the baby continued its crying in the room at the end of the corridor, that his right foot would actually need to be *planted* on the floor of the hallway, as it were, in advance of Harold Absalon overtaking him; no: so long as that foot, associated leg and as much, in fact, of the remainder of his anatomy was in a position to block Harold Absalon's passage through the hallway then it was immaterial whether that foot had actually been planted, at that stage, firmly or otherwise, upon the floor of that hallway. The planting of the foot related more, he thought, to the likely subsequent action of moving the left foot in the direction of Isobel Absalon and the room containing the crying child since, without that foundation on the right hand side it would be most difficult to accomplish the subsequent manoeuvre so described.

He realised, as he noticed, he thought, the husband actually starting to move in pursuit of the wife, that he needed to clarify something from earlier: that in saying that the original destination of his right foot was a position adjacent to his left, that this adjacent position should be taken to be to the immediate right of that left foot. He did not want his cadets and any others following him by whatever mysterious means to think that he was suggesting any kind of contortion at this key moment in his investigation. Relieved to have made this clarification, he noticed that his right foot had finally made the switch, mid-air, that he had been hoping for some time that it would make: it moved, following the receipt of its reprogramming, from a generally front-to-back motion to a generally left-to-right motion, as he noticed, with surprise, that Isobel Absalon had disappeared from view in front of him.

38

HOW HAD SOMEONE of his understanding and experience allowed Isobel Absalon to give him the slip, as he thought it was known, in this way? Granted that Isobel Absalon had only momentarily given him the slip, in that he felt sure that she must still be within the building – in the ground-floor room containing the baby. In fact he knew that, in any case, he wasn't using the term 'giving someone the slip' in the textbook fashion that he had been taught: he thought, on reflection, that this expression could only effectively be applied to exterior rather than to interior pursuits. Why was this the case, he wondered, as his right foot continued its left-to-right flight through the air between husband and wife? The reason that it was only really possible to give someone the slip during an exterior pursuit, as he referred to it, related to the much greater possibilities for disappearance in the wider world outside of a building (and in referring to 'the wider world' he was thinking, as the phone commenced another ring-cycle such that it almost disrupted this train of thought, of the world immediately outside the building in question, that is the wider world of the city rather than the even wider world of the countryside around the city). Essentially there were many more nooks and crannies and hiding places in the city, given the higher population density and the number, height, depth and sheer complexity of design of the buildings and other structures that such a high population density necessitated.

This meant that, when one was pursuing someone out in the open, which is another way of saying outside of any building, including the one that he was currently inhabiting in pursuit of the circumstances surrounding the disappearance of his colleague, Marguerite, last seen on the trail of Harold Absalon, the Mayor's transport advisor, who had been missing, that it was easier, he thought, than in the countryside, to give someone the slip – often all that was involved was going around a corner in that densely populated city such that your pursuer lost sight of you for a sufficient duration to enable you to slip away – into a doorway, say, or down an unlikely alleyway, or over a barbed wire fence, such that, on turning the corner your pursuer would not know, out of the many and diverse options that you could have taken in your continued journey, which way you had chosen to travel – all of this on foot of course; this would leave your pursuer with little option but to guess which way you had gone, perhaps based on a hunch which was itself based, perhaps, on experience of pursuit gained over many years – or in our investigator's case over many decades – but it would, at that stage, be no more than a hunch, and at the moment, or thereabouts, that the pursuer, having gone around that corner, continued their journey but not in the same direction as the pursued had taken then it could be said that the pursued had given the pursuer 'the slip'.

This was not, of course, to say that you could not give a pursuer the slip in the countryside: there were ditches, hedgerows, haylofts and numerous other features that one could, of course, use to one's advantage when one was being pursued in the countryside. However, these features were, on the whole, much thinner on the ground, as it were, than the features of the urban environment; similarly there were typically many fewer people in the countryside than in the city which meant that it was less likely that one could use others – similarly dressed, whether by coincidence or by design – as an opportunistic or prearranged decoy to divert the attention of your pursuer to these others to give yourself the opportunity of giving your pursuer the slip. Nor was it to say that the countryside was not a good place to go if you wanted to disappear: in many ways it was a superior place to go than the city under these circumstances (and the phrase 'needle in a haystack' came into his mind at that moment). It could be a superior place to hide than the city for numerous reasons, which included the sheer amount of countryside that there was – the sheer, that is, surface area of the countryside that one's pursuer would need to traverse in searching for you – combined, he thought, as his right foot landed on the floor of the hallway in advance, he thought, of Harold Absalon, with the scarcity of people who lived in these more rural locations, meaning one's pursuer would have fewer people to ask, 'Have you seen this man/woman?' with the concomitant likeness [28] (as before). Furthermore, any response to this and other questions asked of the people local to that environment were less likely to be intelligible to the city sleuth given the unusual accents that were often current in those locales.

Leaving all that aside for now, he returned to the question of why one could not really give someone the slip during interior pursuits (and his mind, largely without his bidding, given the juxtaposition of the words 'slip', 'interior' and the plural 'pursuits', could not help ruing the opportunity of following Isobel Absalon into the first-floor bedroom that he'd

28 I found, as I scanned the microfiche, photo after photo, column after column (mostly of the gossip variety, I would add) linking Knox with Isobel Absalon.

now missed). He realised that in some circumstances it was, of course, possible to give someone the slip during interior pursuits, but that those circumstances did not pertain to the situation that he currently found himself in. The circumstances that were required to make it much more likely that one could give someone the slip during an interior pursuit related, he realised, as another telephone ring-cycle cut in, potentially, again, disrupting his on-going investigation into the disappearance of his colleague, Marguerite, to the size of the building in which one was conducting the interior pursuit: the larger the building, the easier it would be to give someone the slip, he concluded, somewhat abruptly. In other words, the more that the interior of the building in question resembled the 'outside world' as it were, whether in its urban or more rural manifestations, then to that extent, he thought, as he started advancing his left foot as a precursor to pursuing Isobel Absalon, one was more likely to give someone the slip, as Isobel Absalon had done, momentarily, during an interior pursuit. Given the fact that the house that he was currently located within did not resemble the outside world, even though it was quite a sizeable house, meant that he was confident that Isobel Absalon had not, in fact, given him the slip; he was confident, in short, that were he to enter the room that Isobel Absalon had entered that, given the containment naturally afforded by medium-, or even larger-sized residential buildings, he would find Isobel Absalon within that room. It was for this reason that he was confident that Isobel Absalon had not, in fact, given him the slip and that he had used that phrase in error on this occasion.

39

WHY WAS PUTTING one foot in front of the other so hard for him, he wondered, as he put his left foot in front of his right, and then vice versa, repeatedly and at speed, as a means of moving, as quickly as he could, in pursuit of Isobel Absalon and the end, he hoped, of his investigation into the disappearance of Marguerite?

He felt the need to clarify something of this relationship between his feet, as he moved down the corridor in front of me: in what sense, he wondered, could it be said that in approaching the door to the room in question he was doing so by putting one foot in front of the other? Would it not be more accurate to say that in moving to the now ominously quiet room in that house that he was doing so by a means of propulsion that involved putting one front in front of – *and to one side of* – the other? Would it not be much more accurate to record his evidence in that way of the moments leading up to his entry into that fateful room? If so, why had those investigators who had gone before him not used this fuller, more accurate means of recording their movements at key times such as, in his situation, the moments leading to an arrest and possibly a conviction, assuming that Marguerite's disappearance related, in some way, to something criminal involving Harold and Isobel Absalon and perhaps even Richard Knox? [29] Was it the sheer difficulty of

29 The first report I found, which is not to say it is the first there is of course, had them at a polo match. Isobel, beautiful even then, in the first flush of youth, was wearing that sun hat.

using the means of expressing the evidence that had deterred his colleagues, he wondered, as he continued putting one foot in front of, and to the side of, the other, in rapid succession, such that he was already half-way, or thereabouts, down the corridor en route to the open door? Granted it was reasonably straightforward to record the evidence if one left out reference to right or left, as he himself had just done, in noting, in his own mind (this somehow being conveyed to our minds), that he continued his pursuit of Isobel Absalon by putting one foot in front of, and to the side of, the other. He conceded that it was a step in the right direction in that it was at least a fuller description than the one that one often saw – that is the classic 'putting one foot in front of the other'. It had, at least, the merit of indicating that, in propelling oneself forwards in this way, that each of one's feet, as well as moving, alternately, from a position that was behind the other foot to a position that was in advance of that other foot, also occupied a position, given the peculiarities of the human anatomy (and that of other bipeds, note) that was simultaneously to the side of that other foot. To express it in another way, whilst 'putting one foot in front of and to the side of the other' was a more advanced form of descriptive submission, it had the disadvantage of ambiguity in relation to which foot was in front of and to the side of which. Previously in this part of his investigation he had specified that it was his left foot that had been placed in front of a firmly planted right foot – this was at the outset of his pursuit of Isobel Absalon, remember. Whilst this earlier form of expression had the disadvantage of not being clear that the left foot, as well as being in front of the right, was also to one side of the latter, it did at least have the advantage of specifying which foot was which in the important interplay between them.

Now, the more astute amongst us may have identified a way through this impasse: could one not combine the two models, meaning that, in theory, one could have the specificity of the earlier model at the same time as the lengthier descriptiveness of the later model; in combining, in this way, the two means of recording the evidence, the hope would be that the greater length of the latter would dispel the crude linear dimensionality of the former, and that the specifics of the former would rectify the latter's lateral vagueness. He explored this, as he came to a position, through putting his left foot in front of and to the side of his right, and vice versa, repeatedly, of starting to be able to see into the room in question, not that his field of vision yet contained anything that he felt could be used to bring about any sort of final conviction in the Marguerite case; all he could see was the back of a dining room chair illuminated by weak sunlight from a barred window to the left. The way in which he explored the amalgamation of the two modes, or manners, of expression, as he continued propelling himself in the manner described, was by rehearsing the amalgamation in his mind, thus: in moving towards the open doorway and into the room on the other side of it that he suspected contained the final shreds, if one can call them that, of evidence leading to the resolution of the mystery of the disappearance of Marguerite, his investigative colleague, last seen on the trail of Harold Absalon, the Mayor's transport advisor, who had been missing, he would put his right foot (note) in front of, and to the side of his left foot, and vice versa, repeatedly, and in so doing would propel himself forwards. As he continued moving forwards in this manner, he reflected, as more and more of the room came into view and he saw paper and pen, on an uncovered edge of a dining table, that his documentary evidence, even amalgamating the two modes or manners of expression as it now did, still lacked something of the clarity towards which he always strove. Whilst overcoming both linear and lateral limitations of previous models, the added complication of the new mode of expression had imported with it further ambiguity. To what, for instance, did the 'vice versa' now refer? There were, he noted, four variables, namely, left and right, in front of and to the side. When he had used the more straightforward 'putting his left foot in front of his right, and vice versa, repeatedly' to describe his means of progression it had been clear to what the vice versa referred; but the amalgamation of the two modes or manners of expression had brought with it a further two variables – namely 'in front of' and 'to the side of' – such that it was no longer clear to which set of variables the 'vice versa' referred. Nor did the combination of the two systems resolve an ambiguity previously referred to in his evidence,[30] namely, in referring to putting the right foot in front of, and to the side of, the left, to what side of the left foot should the right foot be taken to momentarily reside – the left or the right? When there was only one step to refer to, as in the previous case, this issue could quite easily and satisfactorily be resolved by simply referring to the correct side: thus, as previously, when he had placed his right foot to the side of his left he could simply specify that he had placed the right foot to the right-hand side of that left foot (though he regretted the emergence of the word 'hand' in his evidence at this point – he thought it only served to confuse matters further and resolved to refrain from using it henceforth when working on this part of his inquiry). What he was finding, as he passed through the doorway and I

30 What most disturbed me – appalled me, really – was the fact that he was old enough to be her father.

lost sight of him, was just how difficult it was really to express how he was feeling at that moment. As for me, I must have put my right foot in front of, and to the right of, my left foot, and my left foot in front of, and to the left of, my right foot; I put my right foot in front of, and to the right of, my left foot, and my left foot in front of, and to the left of, my right foot; again, I put my right foot in front of, and to the right of, my left foot, and my left foot in front of, and to the left of, my right foot; and that is how I find myself inside this room, determined, once again, to understand the circumstances of his disappearance.

Acknowledgements

I T IS A privilege and a pleasure to have the great Nicholas Royle as my editor, and Jen and Chris Hamilton-Emery as my publishers – thank you for your boldness, belief and support. Thanks, also, to John Oakey for another stunning cover, to David Rose for the generous and perceptive endorsement, and to Steve Purnell and Bruce Davidson for the day job. An earlier version of Chapter 1 appeared in *gorse*, for which I am grateful to Susan Tomaselli. Thanks to Sanghasiha for our friendship, and our time amongst the bus enthusiasts. And to Danayutta for your kindness, perseverance and patience: heartfelt thanks, and love.

NEW BOOKS FROM SALT

XAN BROOKS
The Clocks in This House All Tell Different Times
(978-1-78463-093-5)

RON BUTLIN
Billionaires' Banquet (978-1-78463-100-0)

MICKEY J CORRIGAN
Project XX (978-1-78463-097-3)

MARIE GAMESON
The Giddy Career of Mr Gadd (deceased) (978-1-78463-118-5)

LESLEY GLAISTER
The Squeeze (978-1-78463-116-1)

NAOMI HAMILL
How To Be a Kosovan Bride (978-1-78463-095-9)

CHRISTINA JAMES
Fair of Face (978-1-78463-108-6)

SIMON KINCH
Two Sketches of Disjointed Happiness (978-1-78463-110-9)

STEFAN MOHAMED
Stanly's Ghost (978-1-78463-076-8)

EMILY MORRIS
My Shitty Twenties (978-1-78463-091-1)

NICHOLAS ROYLE (ed.)
Best British Short Stories 2017 (978-1-78463-112-3)

GUY WARE
Reconciliation (978-1-78463-104-8)

TONY WILLIAMS
Nutcase (978-1-78463-106-2)

MEIKE ZIERVOGEL
The Photographer (978-1-78463-114-7)

RECENT FICTION FROM SALT

GERRI BRIGHTWELL
Dead of Winter (978-1-78463-049-2)

NEIL CAMPBELL
Sky Hooks (978-1-78463-037-9)

DAVID GAFFNEY
More Sawn-Off Tales (978-1-78463-099-7)

SUE GEE
Trio (978-1-78463-061-4)

CHRISTINA JAMES
Rooted in Dishonour (978-1-78463-089-8)

V.H. LESLIE
Bodies of Water (978-1-78463-071-3)

ROBIN INCE, JOHNNY MAINS (eds.)
Dead Funny: Encore (978-1-78463-039-3)

WYL MENMUIR
The Many (978-1-78463-048-5)

STEFAN MOHAMED
Ace of Spiders (978-1-78463-067-6)

ALISON MOORE
Death and the Seaside (978-1-78463-069-0)

ALISON MOORE
The Pre-War House and Other Stories (978-1-78463-084-3)

NICHOLAS ROYLE (ed.)
Best British Short Stories 2016 (978-1-78463-063-8)

ANNA STOTHARD
The Museum of Cathy (978-1-78463-082-9)

STEPHANIE VICTOIRE
The Other World, It Whispers (978-1-78463-085-0)

PHIL WHITAKER
Sister Sebastian's Library (978-1-78463-078-2)

This book has been typeset by
SALT PUBLISHING LIMITED
using Neacademia, a font designed by Sergei Egorov
for the Rosetta Type Foundry in the Czech Republic.
It is manufactured using Creamy 70gsm, a Forest
Stewardship Council™ certified paper from Stora Enso's
Anjala Mill in Finland. It was printed and bound by
Clays Limited in Bungay, Suffolk, Great Britain.

LONDON
GREAT BRITAIN
MMXVII